"A SUREFIRE WINNER."
—MIRANDA JAMES

TOTALLY PAWSTRUCK

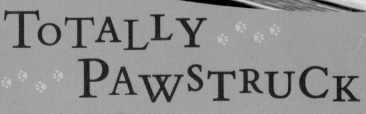

Sofie Ryan

NEW YORK TIMES
BESTSELLING AUTHOR OF
UNDERCOVER KITTY

BERKLEY

$8.99 USA
$11.99 CAN

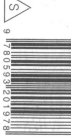

ISBN 978-0-593-20197-8

TOTALLY
PAWSTRUCK

A SECOND CHANCE CAT MYSTERY

Sofie Ryan

BERKLEY PRIME CRIME
New York

BERKLEY PRIME CRIME
Published by Berkley
An imprint of Penguin Random House LLC
penguinrandomhouse.com

Copyright © 2022 by Darlene Ryan
Excerpt from *Curiosity Thrilled the Cat* by Sofie Kelly © 2011 by
Penguin Random House LLC
Penguin Random House supports copyright. Copyright fuels creativity, encourages
diverse voices, promotes free speech, and creates a vibrant culture. Thank you for buying
an authorized edition of this book and for complying with copyright laws by not
reproducing, scanning, or distributing any part of it in any form without permission.
You are supporting writers and allowing Penguin Random House to continue to
publish books for every reader.

BERKLEY and the BERKLEY & B colophon are registered trademarks and BERKLEY
PRIME CRIME is a trademark of Penguin Random House LLC.

ISBN: 9780593201978

First Edition: February 2022

Printed in the United States of America
1   3   5   7   9   10   8   6   4   2

TOTALLY
PAWSTRUCK

Chapter 1

I was running behind, so it didn't help that when I walked into the bathroom I discovered Elvis was in the shower.

"What are you doing?" I asked. At this time of day he was usually sprawled in front of the bedroom TV waiting for *Jeopardy!* to come on.

Elvis didn't so much as glance in my direction. He just continued washing his face as though I weren't there.

So I was getting the silent treatment.

"Your dinner is in the kitchen," I said. I thought that would get a reaction—Elvis was very particular about mealtime—but his gaze didn't dart in my direction for even a moment.

I was out of patience and getting tight on time. I leaned into the shower, picked him up off the floor and then set him down on the fuzzy bath mat—which was easy, because he was, after all, a small, albeit very obstinate, black cat and *not* the King of Rock and Roll.

He narrowed his green eyes at me and gave an indignant meow.

"You know the rules," I said. "Showers are five minutes or less." I pointed a finger at him. "And you better not have used all the hot water."

The cat's response was to flick his tail at me as he stalked from the bathroom—his way, I suspected, of saying he didn't appreciate my humor.

I pulled my hair up into a high ponytail so it wouldn't get wet, turned on the taps and stepped into the shower, letting the hot water unkink the knots in my shoulders. I was grateful that I'd taken Mr. P.'s recommendation on which low-flow showerhead to buy. Alfred Peterson was a true renaissance man. He looked like someone's kindhearted grandpa, but he brewed the best coffee I'd ever tasted, he read extensively and widely and there wasn't a computer system anywhere that he couldn't hack his way into. The last attribute still made me nervous. Mr. P. was also a private investigator, duly licensed by the state of Maine. On occasion that made me a little nervous, too.

When I got back to the bedroom I found Elvis still washing his face, settled in on what had been my favorite chair before he claimed it. I pulled on a pair of jeans and a soft pink sweater that had been a Christmas gift from Rose, who insisted the color brought out the pink in my cheeks.

"It gives you a little glow," she'd said, reaching over to pat my cheek.

Rose and Mr. P. were . . . in a relationship was the best way I'd come up with to describe the two of them. I'd called him her boyfriend once and she'd shaken her head at me. "That makes us sound like a couple of teenagers making out in the backseat of a car." Mr. P. had smiled and raised one eyebrow at her comment. Rose's own cheeks had turned a glowy shade of pink, and I had immediately decided this was not a conversation I wanted to continue.

Rose may have been a very practical woman but she did have a romantic streak. She and her band of merry matchmakers—aka her friends Charlotte, Liz and Isabel, my grandmother—had made a valiant effort to get me together with Charlotte's son, Nick, who was one of my oldest and best friends, but there was just no spark there. Now, much to my amusement and his frustration, all four of them were trying to find someone for Nick.

In some ways I was hoping they did somehow succeed. I loved Nick the way I loved my brother, Liam, and I wanted to see him with someone who was, as Rose put it, the peanut butter to his jelly. When I had pointed out that not everyone liked that combination Rose had beamed and said, "Exactly." And once again I'd decided that was not a conversational road I wanted to start down.

"Nick spends too much time working," I said to Elvis as I pulled the elastic from my hair.

The cat looked up from his face washing, one paw paused in the air. His whiskers twitched.

"Yes, I know it's none of my business."

He murped his agreement and went back to his beauty routine.

I brushed my hair, added mascara and a berry-colored lip gloss and decided that was enough. I made sure the timer was set on the TV so Elvis could watch *Jeopardy!* and I bent down to stroke the top of his head. "I won't be late," I said.

I wrapped the thick, black scarf Rose had knit for me around my neck and pulled on the matching beanie as well. I decided to wear my quilted jacket and an extra pair of socks in my lace-up boots because January in North Harbor, Maine, had only two temperatures: cold and colder.

My breath hung in the frosty air as I started my SUV. I nudged down the cuff of my glove and checked my watch. I'd be only a couple of minutes late getting to The Black Bear pub, where I was meeting Jess. It had been a cold, snowy winter so far with way too many big storms—even for Maine—that had started way back in early November. Jess and I had had our plans to get together derailed twice by the snow and I had sworn to her that we were having dinner even if I had to snowshoe down to the pub. I had gotten home later than I'd planned thanks to a group of snowboarders who had arrived at my repurpose store, Second Chance, in three SUVs just as we were about to close for the day.

I'd always had a pretty much stereotypical image of a snowboarder being, for the most part, someone under the age of thirty who called everyone "dude." These people challenged that narrow-minded generalization the moment they came through the door talking about how great the snow had been. They were all in their mid-forties to early fifties and I didn't hear anyone use the word "dude."

I sold a stack of old 45s, along with a very nice

Fender amp from the 1990s to one of the men, who explained he was a collector. One of the women bought a handmade guitar that I had absolutely no backstory on other than the fact that it had been found in an actual chicken coop. I liked the look in her eyes as she strummed the strings. The fact that I couldn't tell her who had made the guitar or how old it was didn't bother her. "I just like thinking about all the possibilities," she said with a grin.

The rest of the group pretty much decimated the selection of band T-shirts that I had found at a swap meet just across the border in St. Stephen, New Brunswick, right before Christmas, and Elvis, as usual, got lots of attention.

When I got to The Black Bear, Jess was already there, deep in conversation with Sam, who owned the place. Sam Newman had been my dad's best friend and he'd made a point of staying in my life after my father died. Jess smiled when she caught sight of me and Sam turned with a smile as well. He was tall and lean. His shaggy hair was a mix of blond and white, as was his beard. His dollar-store reading glasses were perched on the end of his nose. I gave him a hug. As usual he smelled of coffee and Old Spice aftershave. Sam was the reason I had Elvis. He'd discovered the cat wandering around the waterfront and started feeding him. He'd even given the cat his name, insisting the feline liked the King's music over the Rolling Stones.

"Your hands are cold, kiddo," he said, wrapping his own hands around my icy fingers.

"Cold hands—"

"—warm heart," Sam finished.

I smiled at him.

He rubbed my hands for a minute before he let them go. They were already warmer.

"I need to get back to work," he said. "I'll send a waiter over." He raised an eyebrow. "I'm assuming I'll see both of you for the jam on Thursday."

"Absolutely," Jess said.

I nodded. "I'll be here." Jess and I were regulars at Thursday Night Jam, also known just as the jam, at The Black Bear. The house band, led by Sam, played classic rock and roll, and anyone could sit in for a song or a set or the whole night.

"I'll see you then," Sam said. He gave my arm a squeeze and headed in the direction of the kitchen.

"It's so good to see you in person," I said to Jess.

"You too," she said. She had already gotten to her feet and now she came around the table and gave me a hug. "I was ready to make a pair of snowshoes from duct tape and my vacuum cleaner hose if we had to cancel again."

Jess and I had been friends since she answered my ad for a roommate back when we were in college. She'd actually done more than answered my ad: She'd taken it off the bulletin board where I'd stuck it so no one else could call me before she did.

I got a mental image of her making her way down to the pub on homemade snowshoes. She was five foot nine in her stocking feet and since she usually wore heels she seemed taller than that. "Not the worst idea you've ever had," I said with a grin. "And winter's not over yet." I started unwinding my scarf from around my neck.

Jess caught one end of it. "Oh, I like this," she said. "It's so, so soft."

I nodded. "I know. It's not itchy at all. Rose made it for me."

Jess ran her fingers over the textured pattern. "Do you think she could teach me how to make one?"

"If Rose can teach me how to cook, she can teach you how to knit a scarf," I said.

"If Rose can teach you how to cook, she can teach anything to anyone."

I nodded. "Pretty much."

Jess grinned and gave my arm a squeeze before she sat down again.

I unzipped my coat and hung it on the back of my chair, stuffing my scarf in one of the coat sleeves so it wouldn't end up on the floor.

Our waiter arrived just as I sat down. We listened to the specials and settled on the shepherd's pie and cranberry carrot salad and big mugs of coffee.

Jess leaned back in her chair. Her long, dark hair was pulled back in a messy bun and she brushed a loose strand back off her face. "So, what's been happening at the shop?"

I told her about the snowboarders.

"You actually sold that guitar from the chicken coop? And you told the person where it came from?"

I nodded. "Plus, we sold the rest of those shirts we got at the swap meet. And the two quilts you made from that bin of fabric from the flea market."

"That reminds me, I'm working on two more quilt tops," she said. "But it's going to take me a while. The store has been a lot busier than January usually is, and I'm redoing a wedding dress—grandmother handed down to granddaughter. It needs a lot of work." Jess was part owner of a popular clothing shop on the waterfront.

She was also a very talented seamstress. She could and did do everything from hemming a pair of jeans to designing and making some gorgeous wedding gowns. But what she liked best was reworking vintage clothing from the 1950s through the '70s. Just about everything she restyled that she didn't wear herself ended up in her shop.

The waiter came back with our coffee. After Jess had doctored hers, she took a sip and then folded her hands around the mug. "Cool thing happened this afternoon," she said. "One of the costume people from that movie that's filming down in Portland came in and bought two of my jackets and a vintage pair of Levi's that I had done some embroidery on."

"Your clothes are going to be in a movie. Jess, that's wonderful!" I said.

"Maybe." She shrugged as though what she'd told me wasn't a big deal. "Just because the designer bought something doesn't mean it's going to show up onscreen."

I looked at her for a long moment. One side of her mouth twitched and then she grinned. "Okay, it is pretty exciting."

"We have to go see the movie when it comes out."

"I looked around online, and it's a romantic comedy with Jennifer Lawrence and Leslie Odom Jr." She held up one finger. "And wait for it . . . Steven Tyler!"

"You are making that up," I said, glaring across the table at her.

Jess put one hand flat on her chest. "I swear on all that is righteous in rock and roll that I am not."

"Steven Tyler is within driving distance of North Harbor," I said slowly.

"Not at the moment, but he will be in less than a month. I see a road trip in your future." Jess tried to keep a straight face but it didn't last long.

"I still have scars from the last road trip that involved Steven Tyler."

I had been thirteen and my friend Michelle and I wanted to go see Aerosmith in concert in Portland. Gram, Rose, Liz and Charlotte had taken us in Liz's big Lincoln Continental. During "Walk This Way," Tyler came down off the stage. He was just a few feet away from us and I was so excited I could barely breathe. Until he started dancing with Rose.

"They were all but doing a bump and grind," I reminded Jess, who had heard the story more than once over the years. "And then she kissed him—and not a grandmotherly kiss on the cheek. There's video of the whole thing floating around on the internet somewhere."

"I keep meaning to google that," Jess said.

I stabbed a finger in her direction. "Fine. You can drive Rose to Portland if she finds out Steven Tyler is there."

"I'm game." She got a sly look in her blue eyes. "For the record, I'm a pretty darn good kisser, too."

I pressed the heels of both hands over my eyes. "Great! You and Steven Tyler in a lip-lock. Now there's an image I'm not going to get out of my head anytime soon."

I was saved from any more discussion of kissing aging rock stars by the arrival of our food.

"Do Nancy Drew and her crew have a case at the moment?" Jess asked after trying the shepherd's pie and nodding in satisfaction.

"They just finished one," I said.

Not only was Mr. P. a licensed private investigator, Rose was almost ready to be licensed herself. The two of them, along with Liz and Charlotte, ran an investigation business, Charlotte's Angels, or the Angels for short. They had fallen into their first case when a friend of Charlotte became a murder suspect. They turned out to be pretty good at digging up the truth. More cases had followed. Rose had explained their success by saying, "No one really pays any attention when old people ask questions. Most of the time they don't pay any attention to us at all."

"A man who was one of Charlotte's students was looking for the foster mother who took care of him for six months when he was just a little guy," I said. "He felt that she'd changed his life in the short time he lived with her. The relevant records had been destroyed in a fire, and all Jordan could remember was the park near his foster mother's house."

"They found her, didn't they?" Jess asked.

I nodded. "Yes, they did." I had been with Rose and Mr. P. when they'd given Jordan Thomas the good news. A lump in my throat formed as I remembered the look on his face. "Mr. P used old maps and photos and found the school playground that Jordan had remembered as a park. And Rose and Charlotte figured out that the foster mother was actually quite a bit younger than he'd thought—you know how kids see everyone over thirty as old. It was a happy ending all around."

"They're good at what they do."

"On the surface it seems like they shouldn't be. None of them worked in law enforcement. But they shove all the stereotypes about seniors out the window."

Jess laughed as she speared some of her salad. "Rose and Mr. P. certainly do."

"They're planning a romantic Valentine's Day," I said. "Rose is hiding a fondue pot at my place and Mr. P. is hiding a bottle of wine."

"What are you and Mac doing?" Jess asked.

"Valentine's Day is just a commercialized holiday that puts way too much pressure on men and women to come up with the perfect romantic gesture." I made little air quotes when I said "romantic."

She gave a snort. "In other words: You don't have a clue."

I flushed and ducked my head for a moment. "Okay, I don't," I said. "But that doesn't mean what I just said isn't true."

Our waiter arrived then and refilled our coffee cups.

"There's nothing wrong with Valentine's Day," Jess said. "It's a day about love and chocolate, and neither one is a bad thing in my book." She gestured at me with her fork. "And this is the first Valentine's Day that you and Mac are a couple. You can't just ignore the day."

I automatically smiled the way I always did when someone said Mac's name or when he walked into the room or when I thought about him. Mac and I had started out as friends. He was the first person I'd hired for Second Chance. Over time that friendship had turned into something else.

"You have to celebrate in some way," Jess continued. "First of all, because you get that goofy look on your face whenever his name comes up. And second—and way, way more important—if Rose and Liz and the others find out you have no plans"—she held out both hands in a ta-da gesture—"they will make some for you."

I blew out a breath. "They will, won't they?"

"Oh yeah." Jess's head was nodding like a bobble-head doll. "Remember when Rose decided to use Mac to get information from that bartender and she made him change his shirt because she thought it didn't showcase his assets?"

I laughed, remembering the confusion on Mac's face.

"Do you really want to see what she'd pick to show-case his assets for you?"

I raked a hand back through my hair. "Truthfully, part of me thinks it would take the pressure off and the rest of me suddenly has heartburn."

We shared a piece of chocolate cake with peanut butter icing for dessert while swapping stories of past Valentine's celebrations. We were still laughing about failed romantic gestures after we'd said good night to Sam and started walking to my car.

"He made you tomato soup for Valentine's Day because it was red?" I asked as Jess related a Valentine's Day blind-date story.

"And he cut the grilled cheese sandwich into a heart shape. That's kind of romantic."

I bumped her with my shoulder and shook my head. "No, it isn't."

"Hey, he brought me a box of heart-shaped chocolates the next day."

"Because he forgot to give them to you the day before? Not exactly romantic," I said.

"Actually it was because they were seventy-five percent off once it was the fifteenth."

I laughed and Jess shook her finger at me in mock annoyance. "It's not like *you've* never bought one of those boxes on the day after Valentine's."

"I absolutely have," I agreed. "For myself. Not for someone whose assets I was hoping to see."

We leaned against each other in a heap of giggles as we turned the corner. I was the one who straightened up and stopped laughing first.

I was the one who saw it first: Stella Hall standing over a body lying half in the street.

Chapter 2

There was blood on Stella's hands and a small smear of it on her light brown coat. She was holding some kind of glass ball, which looked to have blood on it as well.

I touched her arm. "Stella, are you all right?" I asked.

She seemed to be in shock. She was alarmingly pale, even in what little pink-tinged light that came from the nearby streetlamp. Stella Hall was a tiny, round woman in her early seventies, maybe five feet tall in her shoes. She had keen blue eyes and soft white hair. She could be a little plainspoken at times, but I knew from experience that she had a very kind heart. I had originally gotten to know Stella when she'd hired us to clear out her late brother's house and sell his furniture at the shop.

"Talk to her. I don't think that blood is hers but she could be hurt," I said to Jess in a low voice. "I need to . . ." I gestured in the direction of the body.

Jess nodded. She spoke softly to Stella and put one

hand on her shoulder. Stella didn't respond at all. I wasn't sure our presence had registered with her yet.

I crouched down next to the body. It was a man in a dark wool dress coat with what looked like a cashmere scarf at his neck. The top half of his body was lying in the street while his legs were splayed out on the narrow sidewalk. There was some blood pooled on the pavement by the back of his head. His eyes were closed.

The man was Vincent Swift, I realized. I didn't know him personally but I knew who he was. Most people in town would. The Swifts had lived in North Harbor for generations and had always been involved in the community. I knew Mr. Swift was in his seventies. Had he had a heart attack or a stroke, collapsed and hit his head? He wasn't moving.

I leaned over and checked for a pulse. To my relief I found one, albeit very weak. Swift was breathing but they were faint, shallow breaths. I loosened his coat and the scarf around his neck, hoping that might help.

Jess had her phone out. Her other hand was on Stella's shoulder. Stella hadn't said a word in response to Jess's questions and I noticed the hand still holding the glass ball was trembling.

"He's alive," I said, turning to look up at them. "But I don't know for how long."

Jess nodded and I heard her pass on the information to the 911 operator.

The injury to the back of Swift's head didn't seem to be still bleeding and I didn't want to make things worse by moving him to check it. I leaned over a little closer and listened to his breathing again. One of the man's hands lay over his midsection, and I covered it with my own. "Hang on, help is coming," I said. I didn't know what else to do.

I looked over my shoulder at Jess again. "It's not good."

"The ambulance is on the way," she said. She leaned closer to Stella so she was directly in the older woman's line of vision. Stella gave her head a little shake. She said something to Jess that I didn't catch.

And then I heard the sirens. I gave Vincent Swift's hand a gentle squeeze, hoping it would let him know he wasn't alone.

It was maybe two more minutes before the ambulance pulled up but it felt a lot longer than that. I recognized one of the paramedics. "Sarah?" he said, his gaze narrowing in surprise as he kneeled down next to me.

"Hey, Danny," I said.

Danny Kincaid was of average height with dark red hair worn long on the top and cropped close on the sides. He had deep green eyes and a playful smile, although he wasn't smiling now. "What's going on?" he asked.

I pushed my hair back off my face. "We—Jess and I—were coming from The Black Bear. We came around the corner and he was just lying here." I gestured over my shoulder. "I think Stella found him. Stella Hall. I'm pretty sure she's in shock."

Danny's partner, a tall woman with choppy blond hair, was checking on Stella.

I looked down at Vincent Swift. "He has a pulse

and he's breathing but he hasn't moved or opened his eyes. I think he hit the back of his head. I loosened his coat and his scarf hoping it might help him breathe better. I didn't move him or anything."

Danny nodded. "Okay. I've got this."

I got to my feet and took several steps backward.

"I'm all right," I heard Stella say haltingly to the other paramedic. "Please . . . just help Vincent." Jess had one arm around Stella's shoulder. Stella was huddled into her caramel-colored wool coat, the collar turned up and her scarf pulled snug around her neck. At least her color was a little better now. She was a strong woman but it had to have been a shock to come around the corner alone and stumble over Vincent Swift's body.

Stella's parents had both come from large families and she seemed to be connected to pretty much everyone in North Harbor. It would have surprised me to find out that she *didn't* know Swift. No wonder she'd been so rattled. I felt a little shaky myself.

I put a hand on Stella's arm. She turned her head and looked at me. "He's not . . . ?" The end of the sentence trailed into silence.

I shook my head. "No. He's alive," I said.

She swallowed and nodded. "Good."

"Stella, what happened?" I asked, keeping my voice low so the paramedics couldn't hear us.

She cleared her throat before she answered. "I was walking home and I saw this ball rolling down the sidewalk toward me." She held up the glass sphere, which was still in her hand. "I picked it up and then I . . . I saw him just lying there. For a moment I wasn't even sure I was looking at a real person. Then all of a sudden you two were . . . here."

"Did you see anyone else?" Jess asked.

Stella shook her head. "I didn't see anyone."

I looked around now, hoping I'd spot some kind of clue as to what had happened. There had been no one ahead of Jess and me on the sidewalk and I couldn't see any footprints in the few patches of snow. I didn't remember hearing voices or even footsteps other than our own and no one else had left the pub when Jess and I did. We had passed several people on the boardwalk, but all of them had been headed in the opposite direction. I wondered where Vincent Swift had been coming from. And Stella.

Before I could ask her, a police car pulled to the curb on the other side of the street and an officer got out. He surveyed the entire area before he took a step away from the vehicle. The first thing he did was walk over to the two paramedics. He had a brief conversation with Danny, who continued to work as they talked.

After a minute or so the officer came over to us. "I'm Officer Stephenson. One of you called 911?"

Jess nodded. "I'm Jess Callahan. I did."

"What happened here?"

She gave a slight shrug. "I don't know."

I gestured from myself to Jess. "We had dinner at The Black Bear. We were walking back to my SUV." I pointed at it parked up the street.

"And you are?" the officer asked.

"Sarah Grayson," I said. "We came around the corner and found Stella and Mr. Swift."

"Is he a friend of yours?"

I shook my head. "No, not personally. But I recognized him right away." Almost anyone who had grown up in North Harbor or had spent any amount of time in town would have known it was Vincent Swift lying in the street. I thought he very much resembled British actor Sir Ben Kingsley. Swift had the same smooth scalp and the same facial hair and piercing gaze, although his dark eyes lacked Kingsley's warmth. He was, like the actor, slightly below average height but Vincent Swift always commanded attention when he walked into a room. The word that most often came up with respect to the man was "arrogant," and from what I had heard, it seemed to be accurate.

The officer glanced around the street again before he spoke. "What did you do next?"

"Jess made sure that Stella was okay, and I checked on Mr. Swift. He was alive and so I stayed next to him to make sure that didn't change."

"Did you see anyone or hear anything?"

I shook my head again. "No."

He looked at Jess.

"No," she said.

The officer then turned his attention to Stella. "Stella Hall," she said before he could ask.

He gave a small nod of acknowledgment. "Ma'am, had you and Mr. Swift been out together?"

Stella laughed, a harsh sound that was more like a bark with no real humor in it. "No, we most certainly were not," she said.

Jess gave me a look I couldn't read.

"We had been at the library for a board meeting," Stella continued. "We're both board members." She repeated what she'd told Jess and me: She was walking home; she saw the glass sphere rolling down the street and picked it up. Then she discovered Swift half lying in the street. "I was . . . I was shocked. For a moment I wasn't sure I was looking at a real person. Before I could do anything, Sarah and Jess came around the corner."

"Did you see or hear anyone or anything?" the officer asked.

"Nothing," she said. "I don't understand what Vincent was even doing here. His driver always picks him up."

"Driver?" The policeman frowned.

Stella looked down at the glass sphere in her hand. "He was in a car accident. It must be a couple of years ago now. He doesn't drive anymore."

I remembered that accident. Vincent Swift's godson had been driving the older man's car. Both of them had been injured and the young man's girlfriend had been killed.

The officer put on a pair of disposable gloves and took the glass ball from her. "All three of you need to wait here for now," he said. He turned back to the paramedics, seeming to take it for granted that we would follow his instructions.

The paramedics had Vincent Swift on a stretcher. The police officer said something to Danny. I saw Danny nod. I couldn't hear what he said. The officer returned to us. "Do any of you know of anyone who would want to hurt Mr. Swift?" he asked.

Since I didn't know the man, I had no idea if he had any enemies. I shook my head. So did Jess.

Stella on the other hand, shrugged. "Pretty much everyone who knows him," she said. "Including me."

Chapter 3

At that moment a dark car pulled in behind the police car and Detective Michelle Andrews got out. I felt a little of the tension seep out of my body. Michelle and I were friends. And she knew Stella as well.

The officer pointed a finger at us. "Stay here, please," he said. He crossed the street toward Michelle as the ambulance pulled away, siren wailing.

I turned my attention to Stella. "Okay, what did that mean?" I said.

Her eyes had followed the ambulance but now she pulled her gaze back to me. "What did what mean?" she asked.

"When that police officer asked if we knew anyone who might have wanted to hurt Vincent Swift you said 'pretty much everyone who knows him.' *Including you.*"

"I wasn't going to lie," Stella said. Her chin came up and her voice had a bit of a defensive edge.

"No one is saying you should," Jess said. "But I

don't think it was such a good idea to offer yourself up as a suspect."

Stella's blue eyes narrowed. "Wait a minute. What do you mean by suspect? Are you saying you think I'm the reason Vincent collapsed?"

My hand was still on her arm and I gave it a squeeze. "No. Jess and I know you. We know you wouldn't hurt anyone." I tipped my head in the direction of the officer across the street, who was still talking to Michelle. "But that police officer doesn't know you. And you do have blood on your hands and your coat."

"Because I picked up that glass ball. What was Vincent even doing with it?"

Jess and I exchanged a look and I shook my head slightly.

"I saw that," Stella said. "Both of you, stop dancing all around the farm. What aren't you saying? Vincent had a heart attack and hit his head on the curb. Didn't he?"

I hesitated for a moment. I didn't want to answer the question, but Stella seemed more like herself now. I knew Michelle was going to walk over and start asking questions of her own in the next couple of minutes and I didn't want Stella to be blindsided.

"His head wasn't anywhere near the curb," I said.

Stella closed her eyes for a moment and raised one hand as though she was going to press it against her mouth.

Jess caught her wrist. "They're going to want to look at your hands," she said.

Stella frowned at her. "Why?"

Jess released her grip and Stella dropped her arm.

"Why will the police want to look at my hands?" Stella said more insistently. "Are you saying you think I did something to Vincent?"

I was shaking my head before she got the words out. "No."

"But you think somebody did."

My hands were cold and I jammed them in my pockets. "I don't know. Maybe."

"Yes," Jess said.

Stella turned to look at Jess as I shot her a warning look but Jess was having none of it. "Like Sarah said, the man didn't hit his head on the curb. The whole top half of his body was lying in the street. There was blood on the back of his head. I saw it. You had to have seen it. And there was enough blood on that glass sphere for you to get it all over your hands." She glanced across the street where Michelle and the officer were still talking. "I know you didn't bash Mr. Swift in the head, but you do have blood on your hands and your fingerprints are on that ball. Think about how it looks."

"In other words, stop talking."

Jess nodded. "Yes."

"Michelle is going to have a lot of questions for you," I said. Out of the corner of my eye I saw her coming toward us. "Call Josh Evans before you answer them."

Stella didn't look at me. Her mouth moved but no words came out.

Michelle joined us then. She was wearing a dark blue quilted jacket with a hood and a pair of heavy

L.L. Bean snow boots. Her red hair was pulled back into a ponytail and she also wore a dark blue knit beanie that I recognized as Rose's handiwork.

She smiled at us but turned her attention to Stella. "First of all, I just want to double-check. Officer Stephenson said you weren't hurt. Is that right?"

"I'm fine," Stella said. "Thank you for asking."

Michelle nodded. "Good." She looked at me. "Sarah, I'm going to start with you."

"Okay," I said.

Her gaze shifted back to Stella and Jess. "It's really cold out here. Why don't the two of you go wait in Officer Stephenson's cruiser?"

Stella's chin jutted out again. "I don't mind the cold."

Jess's nose was red and she'd pulled up the hood of her jacket. I knew she had to be cold. I was. But she just smiled. "We're all right," she said. "But thanks."

Michelle led me a few steps away so we were out of earshot of Stella and Jess. "She's stubborn," she said.

"You mean Stella? Yeah. She is. Look who her friends are: Rose. Gram. Liz." I ticked them off on my gloved fingers.

Michelle rolled her eyes. "Good point." Her expression turned serious. "So, what happened here?"

I told her what I'd told Officer Stephenson.

"Did you see anyone else?"

I shook my head. "I don't remember anyone walking ahead of us and the only person I saw when we turned the corner—other than Vincent Swift, who was lying in the street—was Stella."

"What was Stella doing?"

"She wasn't doing anything," I said. "She was just standing there."

"She wasn't bending over the body? She wasn't doing CPR?"

I blew out a breath and it hung in the icy air for a moment. "She was in shock. Her color was awful. Her face was gray." I sounded a little defensive, I realized.

She held up one hand. "Okay. So, what did you do?"

I explained how I'd checked Mr. Swift for a pulse while Jess kept an eye on Stella and called for help.

"Did Stella say anything to you?"

"She said she came around the corner and there was a glass ball rolling down the sidewalk toward her. She went to pick it up and she saw Mr. Swift's body."

"So she was still holding the ball when you found the two of them?"

"Yes."

"And she had blood on her hands?"

I cocked my head to one side. "C'mon Michelle, you saw Stella's hands. You know there's blood on them. And Officer . . ." I gestured with one hand trying to remember the man's name.

"Stephenson," she said.

"Stephenson," I repeated. "He took the ball away from her. He had to have told you that."

Michelle stuffed her hands in her pockets. "I'm just trying to find out what you saw."

I struggled to keep the irritation out of my voice. Michelle was a good cop. A *fair* cop. She wouldn't try to railroad Stella. "I saw a man lying on the ground and a woman in shock."

"Okay." She almost smiled. "I'm going to talk to Jess for a minute and then the two of you can go."

"What about Stella?"

"You know how these things work, Sarah. I need to question Stella. My forensics people need to swab her hands and take some photographs."

"You know Stella," I said. "You know she didn't . . . do anything."

"I'm not making any judgments. I'm just gathering the facts." She pulled her phone out of her pocket and checked the screen. "I'll have Officer Stephenson take Stella over to the police station," she said, without looking up from her phone. "It'll probably be half an hour or so before I'll get there. You can tell that to Josh."

"Thank you," I said softly.

She looked up and smiled. "Just doing my job."

While Michelle questioned Jess, I called Josh; I had his law office and cell numbers in my phone. He'd bailed Rose and crew out of more than one sticky situation, and I knew Josh would keep Stella from getting herself in trouble. When he answered I explained briefly what had happened and he asked to speak to Stella. I handed her the phone and moved a few steps away so I couldn't hear their conversation.

It was brief. Less than a minute later Stella walked over to me and handed me my phone. "You didn't trust me to call Joshua myself," she said.

"Would you have?"

She laughed, giving her head a shake. "Child, you are spit out of Isabel's mouth."

Being told I was like my grandmother was always

a compliment in my book. "I hope I am," I said with a smile.

Michelle and Jess rejoined us. "Officer Stephenson is going to drive you to the station now," Michelle said to Stella. "I'll be there shortly."

Stella nodded.

"We can follow you," I offered.

"No need to," Stella said. "But thanks for the offer." She shifted her gaze to Michelle. "My lawyer will be there."

"Go home and get warmed up," Michelle said to Jess and me. "I'll want to talk to both of you tomorrow."

"I'll be working all day," Jess said.

"You know where to find me," I added.

Michelle gestured to Officer Stephenson, who walked over to us as more police vehicles arrived. Jess and I waited until the police cruiser with Stella in the backseat, her eyes focused resolutely straight ahead, pulled away from the curb before we started for my SUV.

Jess climbed in the passenger seat and leaned her head back against the headrest, closing her eyes. I started the engine and cranked up the heat. "I keep thinking I'm going to wake up and this is going to be nothing but a very bad dream," she said.

I pulled off one glove and stuck my hand in front of the heat vent. "I wish you were right."

Jess opened her eyes and turned her head to look at me. "You called Josh Evans, didn't you?"

"I did."

"Good," she said. "I don't think Stella would have."

I exhaled loudly. "I don't think she would have, either. She seems to think the truth will protect her."

"Yeah, well, I think Josh will do a better job." After a short silence Jess spoke up again. "Sarah, how much do you know about the board of directors for the library?"

"I know there is one," I said. "That's pretty much it. Why?"

She sighed softly. "When you have a business that's right downtown you hear all the gossip, even if you don't always want to."

I didn't say anything.

"Like Stella said, both she and Vincent Swift are on the library board," she continued.

I had known that Stella was a board member. I hadn't known Vincent Swift was until Stella told Officer Stephenson they had both come from the meeting. I shifted in my seat so I was facing Jess. "Jess, just spit it out," I said, "whatever it is."

"Stella is one of the newest members and she and Mr. Swift have been butting heads pretty much since her first board meeting. From what I've heard, they've never been on the same side of any issue. Remember when they were going to sell the Sunflower Window from the old library to some person from Singapore?"

"I remember," I said. My grandmother and Liz had joined former judge Neill Halloran in a fund-raising and public relations effort that had resulted in the window remaining in town. "And I know Stella was involved in the campaign to keep the window here, too."

"And Mr. Swift was firmly in the other camp. He

supposedly called the whole fund-raising effort 'misplaced sentimentality.'"

I began to nod my head. "Now that I think about it, I think Liz called him a 'self-important windbag.'"

Jess laughed. "That sounds like something Liz would say." She pulled off her mittens and slid her hands under her thighs to warm them up. "The thing is, Stella and Mr. Swift have had more than one very loud and very public argument about a whole range of things."

"C'mon, Jess," I said, feeling a knot beginning to tighten in my stomach. "You can't honestly think Stella beat Vincent Swift unconscious with that glass ball because they disagreed about selling the Sunflower Window?"

"Of course I don't. But she didn't get along with the man and she had more than enough opportunity to have attacked him. Just because we know Stella didn't try to kill the man doesn't mean the police do."

Chapter 4

I drove Jess home. She leaned over and gave me a hug before she got out. "I'm still glad I got to see you in person," she said. "Let me know if you hear anything, okay?"

"I will," I said. "You'll do the same?"

She nodded. "Absolutely."

I headed home wondering how things were going for Stella at the police station. I realized I'd probably overstepped when I called Josh but I wasn't sorry I'd done so. Stella was honest almost to a fault and I didn't want that to get her in trouble.

Elvis was stretched out on his chair when I got home, one paw over his nose. He lifted his head, tipped it quizzically to one side and meowed softly, almost as though he knew something was up.

I ran my fingers through my hair and yawned. "It's a long story," I said. "I'll tell you over breakfast. Right now all I want to do is have a hot bath and go to bed."

A soak in the tub got rid of the last of the chill I was feeling. I pulled on my favorite plaid flannel pajamas and a pair of fuzzy socks and climbed into bed. I wanted to talk to Mac, I realized. I was feeling unsettled and I knew he'd say something that would put my mind at ease.

He answered on the third ring. "I was hoping you'd call," he said. I could picture him smiling on the other end of the phone and that image made me feel a little better. "How was your evening? How was dinner with Jess?"

"Dinner with Jess was good," I said.

"But something else wasn't?"

I shook my head even though he couldn't see me and slid down on the pillows. "No." I gave him a quick recap of what had happened.

"Vincent Swift is the man Liz and your grandmother clashed with over the Sunflower Window, isn't he?" Mac said.

Word got around. "He is."

"Any relation to Daniel Swift?" Daniel Swift had been involved in one of the Angels' previous cases.

"A third cousin or something like that. Charlotte would know. She knows how everyone is connected to everyone else."

"I'm guessing Vincent Swift and Stella didn't get along any better than he and Liz did," Mac said.

"According to Jess, no, they didn't."

"Sarah, are you certain what happened *wasn't* an accident?"

Elvis gave an inquisitive "mrrr" as though he'd somehow heard Mac's question and wanted to know the answer as well. He was curled up in the chair, front paws tucked under his body as though he were warming them up, listening intently to my side of the conversation.

"I don't see how it could have been," I said. "It's possible Swift slipped on a tiny patch of black ice or suddenly got dizzy, but how did the blood get on that glass ball? And before you ask, aside from the blood by the back of his head, there wasn't any other blood around his body. I looked."

"I trust your judgment," Mac said. "I was just fishing for an explanation that leaves Stella out."

I yawned. "That would be good but for now there isn't one. At least Michelle knows Stella, and Josh is on the case." I yawned again.

"Get some sleep," Mac said. "Things will sort themselves out."

We said good night and I turned off the light. I fell asleep hoping he was right.

There was no sign of Elvis when I woke up the next morning. I padded out to the kitchen to find him sitting on a stool at the counter. He looked expectantly at me. "I'm starting the coffee first," I said.

I poured water into the machine and got out the coffee. This particular blend was Mr. P.'s latest find from a small coffee roaster in northern Maine. It wasn't somewhere I'd expected to find a coffee roaster but I didn't really know much about the process. Mr. P. had ground the beans himself. I had to admit it was excellent coffee. Mr. P. was "educating" my palate, as he put it, when it came to coffee. I was slowly starting to appreciate the nuances of his different finds. For a long time all I'd cared about was that my coffee was strong and hot.

I turned around to look at Elvis. "So will it be seafood or chicken this morning?"

His whiskers twitched as he considered the choices, then suddenly his head swiveled and he stared at the front door. A few seconds later I heard a knock and went to answer it. I had no idea how Elvis could tell someone was about to come to the door. My best guess was that he could somehow feel the vibrations of a person's footsteps out in the hall or possibly hear them. Or maybe he was just psychic.

"You can tell when someone is at the door but you can't start the coffeemaker," I said as I moved past him.

He wrinkled his nose at me.

Rose was standing there holding a bowl that smelled like bacon and sweet potatoes. Not only was she an investigator in training, she also worked for me and she lived in one of the two other apartments in my renovated Victorian. All that togetherness should not have worked. But it did.

"Good morning," she said. "I brought you breakfast." She held out the dish and I took it from her.

Along with the bacon and cubes of roasted sweet potato, there was spinach, chunks of red pepper, a little scrambled egg and some shavings of Parmesan cheese.

"Eat while it's hot," she said, shooing me back inside with one hand.

Rose Jackson was barely five feet tall with short white hair, warm gray eyes and the tenacity of a border collie. Arguing with her was pointless—something I didn't always remember.

I headed for the kitchen to get a fork. Rose followed, closing the door behind her. Once I'd grabbed a fork I settled on the stool next to Elvis. He eyed the bowl, his nose twitching. One of the cat's superpowers may have been the ability to tell when someone was going to knock at the door, but Rose's was knowing what was happening in town pretty much as fast as it happened. She had gotten a mug out of the cupboard and was pouring the coffee. I knew it was for me. Rose was a die-hard tea drinker.

She added cream and sugar and set the cup in front of me. "Thank you," I said. "How did you find out?"

She didn't even try to pretend she didn't know what I was talking about. "Stella, Tabitha, me." She ticked off the names on her fingers. Tabitha Gray lived in the seniors' apartment complex where Rose had lived before she'd moved in with me. Somehow, Tabitha knew what everyone in town was up to—and who they were up to it with.

"Would you like me to give Elvis his breakfast?" Rose asked.

"I can do it," I said, setting my dish on the counter.

"I know you can," she said. "What I asked was if you'd like me to do it."

Why did I suddenly feel like not letting Rose feed my cat would somehow be insulting her? "Well . . . yes, thank you."

She beamed at me. "You're welcome."

Rose and Elvis settled on chicken after she'd read the labels on both cans of food. Once Elvis was eating, Rose washed her hands and then turned to look at me. "They didn't arrest Stella."

"I didn't think they would," I said. "She didn't do anything wrong."

"And you know that doesn't always matter."

I did know that. "What about Vincent Swift?" I took a sip of my coffee.

She shook her head. "I haven't heard anything. I'm hoping no news is good news."

"That would be nice," I said.

"Is there any way what happened could have been an accident?" Rose asked, smoothing the front of her apron.

I put down my fork. I hadn't changed my opinion since Mac had asked me the same question the night before. "I don't think so. Swift was half on the street, half on the sidewalk, lying on his back. His head wasn't anywhere near the curb. If he'd slipped or lost his balance, I think he would have fallen forward, not backward." I took a deep breath and let it out slowly. "And Stella picked up a glass sphere, like a fortune-teller's ball." I held up my hands to give Rose an idea of how big the ball had been. "There was blood on it."

"You think someone hit him with it."

"I think it would be an awfully big coincidence if that blood turns out to belong to someone else."

Rose sighed. "Vincent is . . . the kind of man who has always made more enemies than he did friends."

"When Gram and Liz were working with Judge Halloran to save the Sunflower Window, I remember Liz didn't have anything good to say about him." I picked up my fork again.

"She called him a donkey's backside," Rose said. "Among other things."

I speared a chunk of sweet potato. "If that's all she said, he got off easy."

"I'm sure you know that Stella didn't get along with him any better."

"I heard."

"But she wouldn't have attacked him. Argue with him? Challenge his ideas? Yes. But resort to violence? Never." Rose squared her shoulders as though she was ready to challenge anyone who disagreed with her.

"I know that," I said gently. "And so does Michelle. She knows Stella."

"You're right," Rose said. "Once Vincent regains consciousness, everything will be fine." She smiled at me. "I'm going to finish getting ready for work."

I smiled back at her. "Thank you for breakfast."

"You're very welcome." She patted my arm and left.

I kept the smile on my face until the front door closed. Despite the food I'd just eaten, there was a gnawing feeling in the pit of my stomach. What happened if Vincent Swift didn't regain consciousness?

Rose was waiting when I stepped into the hallway about twenty minutes later. She was wearing a bright red parka and a matching red hat with a fluffy pom-pom. And she was carrying one of her tote bags that had approximately the same capacity as a clown car in the circus.

"Mr. P. isn't coming with us?" I asked.

Most mornings if Rose was headed to the shop with me, so was Mr. P. The Angels' office was located in the converted sunporch at Second Chance. They paid a lot less rent than they would for the same amount of space anywhere else—I didn't want to charge them anything at all, but both Rose and Mr. P. had insisted and it had turned out to be yet another "discussion" I was doomed to lose. And it meant that I knew, for the most part, what their current cases were. It also meant that I often got roped into their investigations.

"Alfred is getting his hearing tested this morning," Rose said.

I frowned as I opened the passenger door for her. "I didn't know he was having problems with his hearing."

"Oh, he's not. He just doesn't want to end up being one of those old people who complain that younger people just don't speak up when they're all but shouting at them."

I smiled. "I don't see that happening."

Rose smiled back at me. "Neither do I, dear. But Alfred likes to be proactive." Elvis hopped up on to the seat and she climbed in after him. I walked around to the driver's side of the SUV.

Rose settled her bag between her feet and buckled her seatbelt. Elvis sat between us. He peered through the windshield for a moment, glanced at me and then looked over his shoulder.

The cat was an opinionated backseat driver. My best guess was that he'd learned the behavior wherever he'd lived before he ended up with me. He'd watch the street attentively and meow indignantly if he felt I'd broken any rules of the road. He'd taken pretty much all the fun out of going past the posted speed limit when I was out on the highway—which was probably a good thing for everyone.

"Do you think you could teach Jess how to knit?" I asked Rose after I'd backed out of the driveway and we were making our way down the street.

"I thought Jess knew how to knit." From the corner of my eye, I could see Rose frowning.

I shook my head. "She doesn't, and she really likes the scarf you made for me."

"I'd be happy to teach her," Rose said. "And that scarf is very easy to make. I'm sure I could teach a chimpanzee how to knit that."

"I'm certain you could," I said, "but right now Jess is the only one who wants to learn."

It was a beautiful morning. There were no clouds in the sky so it was bitingly cold, but the sun was warm and the forecast promised warmer temperatures in the afternoon and no snow for the rest of the week.

North Harbor sits on the midcoast of Maine. "Where the hills touch the sea" is the way it's been described for the past two-hundred-plus years. The town stretches from the Swift Hills in the north to the Atlantic Ocean in the south. Because we're so close to the ocean, we often get hammered by winter storms. Even so, I couldn't imagine living anywhere else.

North Harbor had been settled in the late 1760s by Alexander Swift (Vincent Swift was one of his descendants). The town is full of gorgeous old buildings and quirky small businesses. Several well-known artists live in the area and there are a number of award-winning restaurants. The town's year-round population is just over thirteen thousand people, but that number more than triples in the warm weather with summer residents and tourists.

As a kid I'd spent my summers in North Harbor with my grandmother. It was where my father had grown up, and I didn't want to be anywhere else in the summertime. Once I was old enough I even managed to find myself a summer job here. After college I'd worked in radio, coming back to visit as often as I could. When that job disappeared, I'd come to Gram's to sulk for a while. Instead I'd ended up staying and opening Second Chance. The store was in a redbrick building, built in late 1800s, close to downtown North Harbor. We were a fifteen- to twenty-minute walk from the harbor front and close to the off-ramp from the highway, which meant we were easy for tourists to find and get to.

When we got to the shop, Rose climbed out of the SUV and picked up her tote bag with one hand. She scooped Elvis off the seat with the other.

"Rose, you spoil that cat," I said.

"Me carrying Elvis once in a while is hardly spoiling him." Elvis looked at me with a gleam of smugness in his green eyes.

"And if it is," she continued as we headed across the parking lot to the back door, "then I guess I shouldn't have brought oatmeal raisin cookies because that would mean I'm spoiling you."

"It's not the same thing," I said, hating how petulant I sounded.

Rose's glasses had slid partway down her nose and she looked at me over the top of them before she pushed them up again with one finger. "It's exactly the same thing. You like a cookie on occasion and Elvis likes to be carried on occasion."

We both knew I liked a cookie on pretty much every occasion possible, which was about how often Elvis wanted someone to carry him.

I did the pragmatic thing. I stopped talking.

Mac was waiting in the shop with a large mug of coffee. He lived in a small apartment on the second floor.

"Just what I needed, thank you," I said, taking the heavy stoneware mug from him.

"I'm going to make the tea," Rose said, heading for the stairs. She set Elvis down by the bottom step.

"The kettle should be just about ready to boil," Mac called after her.

She turned and beamed at him. "Thank you. You spoil me." Her gaze flicked to me for a moment and she headed up the stairs.

I blew out a breath and took a sip of coffee.

"Am I missing something?" Mac asked. He was tall and lean with dark skin, dark eyes and muscles in all the right places. He wore his hair cropped close to his scalp. I loved to run my fingers over it.

I shook my head. "No. Rose and my cat have just bested me. Again."

He took the mug out of my hand, set it on the cash desk and wrapped his arms around me. "Does this help?"

"A little," I said.

He kissed the top of my head. "How about this?"

"That's a bit better."

He leaned down and kissed my mouth. "And this?"

"Perfect," I said.

He smiled at me. "Good."

I picked up my mug again. "What's your day look like?" I asked.

In his past life Mac had been a financial planner, but he'd walked away from the job to come to Maine and sail. All summer long he crewed for pretty much anyone who asked. There were eight windjammer schooners that tied up at the North Harbor dock, along with dozens of other boats, so he managed to spend a lot of time on the water. Eventually he wanted to build his own boat. He'd originally come to work for me because he wanted to do something where he could see some progress at the end of the day

"I'm hoping to work on that table you bought from Cleveland."

Cleveland was one of the pickers I bought from regularly. Second Chance was part secondhand shop, part antique store. We carried furniture, dishes, quilts, collectibles and some musical instruments. Many things had been repurposed from their original use, like the teacups we'd used as tiny planters or a chair Mac had turned into a plant stand. Our stock came from a lot of different places: yard sales, flea markets, people looking to downsize and pickers like Cleveland.

"What about you?" Mac said as I took another sip of my coffee.

"There are a couple of chairs I need to paint, and I want to gather up all the old Pyrex dishes we have.

We should put more of them out. As fast as we do, we sell them."

"There's at least one box out in the old garage," he said. "I'll bring it in."

We had turned the former garage into a workspace but we all still referred to it as the "old garage."

"Thanks," I said.

"Have you heard anything from Stella?" Mac asked.

I shook my head. "I haven't, but I do expect to hear from Michelle sometime today. Maybe no news is good news."

Turns out it wasn't.

Stella Hall showed up just before eleven o'clock. I was just coming down the stairs. Mac was carrying a pie safe out for a customer. Rose was organizing the various Pyrex dishes from the box Mac had brought in. The dishes were spread on the top of a long farmhouse table. Mac and I had assembled the piece from two damaged tables we'd salvaged from a garbage pile.

"Do you have a minute?" Stella asked, looking from Rose to me. She was wearing the same caramel-colored jacket she'd had on the night before but the blood had been cleaned off of it.

"Of course," I said.

Rose nodded in agreement.

"Vincent Swift is dead," Stella said. There was no emotion in her voice.

"Damn!" I muttered just under my breath.

Stella looked at Rose. "I want to hire you to find out who killed him."

"Why?" Rose asked. "I didn't think the two of you

were friends. I didn't think you even liked one another."

"We weren't and we didn't," Stella said. "I want to hire you because I'm pretty sure I'm the number one suspect in his death."

Chapter 5

For a moment I just stared at Stella. Rose, on the other hand, was a little less stunned by Stella's words. "What makes you think you're a suspect?" she asked, in the same tone of voice she might have used to say "Please pass the salt."

I finally found my voice. "Did Detective Andrews tell you that?"

Stella shook her head. "No, she didn't. But I could tell by the questions she asked me." She raised one hand. "And don't worry. I didn't answer any question Joshua told me not to."

"I'm glad to hear that," I said. I was also happy that I had followed my impulse to call Josh in the first place.

Rose narrowed her gray eyes. "What kinds of questions did she ask?"

"She wanted to know about any arguments Vincent and I had." Stella gave a humorless snort of laughter. "What didn't the two of us argue about? The man was impossible. He was unwilling to see any perspective other than his own. Do you remember a few years ago when that developer wanted to put condos on that piece of land next to Swift Hills Park?"

"I remember that," I said. My grandmother had been involved with a group that had opposed the development. Most people in town had been happy when Gram's group prevailed.

"You two were on opposite sides of that debate, as I remember," Rose said.

"We still are," Stella said. "I mean, we were. Vincent was floating that whole proposal once again."

Rose stared at her, incredulous. "Again? Why? There was very little support for the idea the last time."

Stella shrugged. "It's just the kind of man he was—totally motivated by self-interest. He was still objecting to the Sunflower Window going in that new apartment building that's going to be built downtown."

"What difference would that make to him?" I asked.

Stella made a dismissive gesture with one hand. "The man was a sore loser. It turns out he had been working on the deal that would have sent the window out of the country, so now his latest thing was insisting it should have been put up for auction to get the most money for the library. Because after all, wasn't encouraging children to read far more important than getting sentimental about that window?"

"What a load of horse manure!" Rose exclaimed. "Every time the reading mentor program looked to expand, Vincent Swift insisted there was no more money in the library budget."

Stella rolled her eyes. "You're not going to like this then. He claimed if the Sunflower Window had been put up for auction at least some of the money could have gone to the mentor project. A program he had previously said was 'superfluous.'"

"If he were alive I would give Vincent Swift a piece of my mind," Rose said. Anger flashed in her gray eyes. As a former teacher, she had a soft spot for the library's reading mentor program.

"So it's safe to say the two of you were pretty much on opposite sides of anything that was happening in town," I said.

Stella nodded. "Yes. And I'm not trying to pass the buck by saying I wasn't the only one. The thing is, I think you know me well enough, Sarah, to know I don't suffer in silence. Vincent and I argued more than once, and several of those arguments were very public."

"Oh, Stella," Rose said softly.

I wasn't exactly surprised. Stella Hall wasn't the type of person to stay silent when she saw someone acting like a bully. I couldn't criticize. It was one of the things I admired about her. Gram had said she'd been the same way with bullies on the playground when they were kids. "Okay, what was the most recent one of those arguments about?"

"The library." She ducked her head and shifted somewhat uneasily from one foot to the other.

I waited. Rose looked like she was about to say something and I made an almost imperceptible shake of my head.

"The library, but money, too," Stella finally said.

"So this had to do with the library budget?" I said.

"Not exactly. We were about to receive a large bequest from the estate of a woman who'd had no family. Most people, when they leave money to the library, specify what they want it used for. She didn't. Several of us wanted to fund a learn-to-read project. It's an idea that's been tossed around for years but there's never been any money to make it a reality."

"It's a good idea," Rose said. "Adults who don't have good reading and writing skills are more likely to be underemployed or not be able to find a job at all, which means they're also more likely to resort to some type of criminal activity just to make ends meet."

"And their children are at greater risk of not finishing school and ending up in the criminal justice system," Stella added. "Making sure a child can read and write well—what better legacy could there be?" She shook her head. "I'm sorry. I'm preaching."

"I take it Mr. Swift didn't agree with you," I said.

The muscles in Stella's jaw tightened. "No, he didn't. He wanted to use the money to buy a collection of historical documents that pertain to the settlement of this area. Guess whose family those documents are primarily about? He kept throwing around that old chestnut 'Those who cannot remember the past are condemned to repeat it.'"

"Spanish philosopher George Santayana," Rose said softly.

I wasn't surprised she knew that.

"The only past Vincent cared about was his own family's," Stella said. "We'd been fighting about it for weeks." She rubbed the bridge of her nose with her thumb and index finger. "More than one board meeting got a little heated. Vincent is—was—a businessman and a financial adviser. He used his so-called expertise to bully most of the other board members. Not me."

I didn't doubt that for a moment, which wasn't going to help Stella.

"I was pretty sure our side had enough votes to prevail, I knew Neill Halloran agreed with me, but I didn't trust Vincent as far as I could throw him. I knew he was trying to provoke me. I think he liked the arguing. I shouldn't have let myself get sucked into it."

"When was your last argument?" Rose asked.

Stella's face got red and she glanced down at her feet for a moment.

My stomach sank and I had to swallow away the sudden sour taste at the back of my throat.

"The night he died," she said in a low voice.

Rose and I exchanged a look. This was not good.

"Vincent and I had . . . words at the meeting. I'm not trying to make excuses for my behavior"—her eyes met mine—"but I was fed up with his attitude and his bullying. I walked out because I was afraid if I stayed I'd slap him. And yes, I know how bad that sounds."

"But you didn't slap him," Rose said. There was sympathy in her gray eyes.

Stella shook her head. "He came out after me but I knew it wasn't a good idea to talk to him then. So I walked around in the stacks downstairs until I cooled off. I had been going back upstairs to confront him but I came to my senses and realized that would just make things worse. I admit I entertained the fantasy of smacking that smug smile right off his face more than once, but I didn't do it. And I didn't kill him."

"I'll have to talk to everyone else before I can say yes . . . or no," Rose said. I couldn't tell what she was thinking from the expression on her face.

"I understand," Stella said. She turned to me. "I'm sorry you and Jess got pulled into this mess."

"That's not on you," I said.

She smiled. "And thank you for calling Joshua. I probably would have made things worse for myself if he hadn't been there at the police station."

"I'll be in touch," Rose said.

Stella nodded then left.

Rose watched her go, a thoughtful expression wrinkling her forehead. After a moment she turned to me. "What do you think?" she asked.

I twisted my watch around my arm. "I think that there are a lot of kids in North Harbor who learned to read because of Stella."

Rose nodded. "I think that Ellie might have lost her four children to foster care, at least temporarily, when she needed that spinal surgery if Stella hadn't gone to take care of them all. Or maybe Ellie would have skipped the surgery and not be walking now."

Ellie Hall was the ex-wife of Stella's nephew. The fact that the couple were divorced didn't matter to Stella. Ellie was still family.

I let out a breath. "Stella is Ellie's aunt by marriage,

and that marriage ended. No one expected Stella to take on looking after those kids and no one would have faulted her if she hadn't."

"Stella holds herself to some pretty high standards," Rose said.

"Those kids think of Stella as their grandmother," I said. "Without her, all they would have is their mother. They love her, and so does Ellie." I thought about my own grandmother. She and Stella had been friends since they were captains of opposing Red Rover teams on the playground. "Are we taking a vote?"

Rose smoothed the front of her apron. "Yes, but if you don't want us to take on the case then I will vote no."

I knew if Rose said no then Mr. P. would as well.

"Why?" I asked.

She reached up and put a hand to my cheek for a moment. "Because you and Jess are involved in this one—on the edges, yes, but there you are nonetheless. You didn't sign on for it and you, especially, don't have to get any more involved than you already are."

I always seemed to get pulled into the Angels' cases whether or not I wanted to be involved. This time I had an out if I wanted to use it.

I didn't. "I vote yes," I said, "and I know Jess would as well."

Rose smiled. "I'll go talk to Alfred. We can see what Charlotte says when she gets here at lunchtime."

I put an arm around Rose's shoulders and gave her a squeeze. "What about Liz?"

Rose made a face like she'd just discovered the

milk for the tea was sour and shook her head. "I'm afraid she's going to take a little convincing. She loathes"—she stopped—"loathed Vincent Swift."

"You can be very persuasive," I said.

She smiled. "Yes, I can."

Mac came in from the workroom just then. He looked at us and his gaze narrowed. "Something's up," he said.

"Vincent Swift is dead," Rose said, her tone matter-of-fact. "And Stella wants to hire us to find his killer." She cocked her head to one side like a curious little bird. "What do you think?"

Mac focused just on me for a moment, and it seemed that there was just a hint of a smile on his face. "I vote yes," he said.

She gave a nod of approval. "So did I." She patted my shoulder. "I'm going to talk to Alfred. I'll be quick."

She headed for the workroom door, reaching out to give Mac's arm a squeeze as she passed him. He walked over to me. "I take it Stella is a suspect in Swift's death," he said.

"She thinks she is and she's probably right. I should check in with Josh and make sure he's okay with the Angels taking Stella on as a client."

Mac nodded. "That's a good idea. It might be worth calling Nick, too. Wouldn't it help if you knew for sure how Swift died?"

"It would help," I said, "but I'm not so sure he'd tell me."

He smiled. "Well, Rose did make him part of the team, and let's face it, Mr. P. has ways of getting that information. If I know that, then Nick definitely does, so as long as it's not privileged information I think he might be willing to share."

His logic made sense. "It can't hurt to try," I said. I rubbed the back of my neck with one hand. "Stella didn't do this."

"I know," Mac said. "All you and Rose and the others have to do is figure out who did."

Liz walked in just after lunch, having driven both Avery and Charlotte to the shop. Avery's nonconformist private school had only morning classes so I'd hired her to work afternoons in the shop—but not, as most people assumed, because she was Liz's grandchild. The prickly teen was surprisingly good with customers, just as I'd suspected she'd be. She was honest without being rude and more than one person had asked specifically for her after their first visit to the shop. Her eclectic sense of what went with what tended to win people over. More than once a customer had purchased a table that Avery had styled along with everything on it *and* then snapped photos from every angle to be able to re-create what she had put together.

Avery had an eye for color and a quirky personal style. She had decided to grow out her last choppy haircut. A stylist had evened the layers and given her long bangs. The style suited her, showing off her high cheekbones. She tended to favor black jeans and dark shirts and her current outside footwear was a pair of black and burgundy L.L. Bean winter "Bean" boots. Inside the shop she wore a vintage pair of black Doc Martens she'd discovered at a flea market she'd gone to with Mac and me.

"Did you really find a dead guy in the street?" she asked as she unwound the long, striped scarf Rose had made for her from around her neck.

"Jess and I did find someone lying in the street," I said. "But he wasn't dead. Not at that point."

"See what happens when you listen in on other people's conversations?" Liz said. "You don't get all the facts.'

Avery leaned over and kissed her grandmother on the cheek. "I could say 'Back at you, Nonna,' but I'm not going to, because that would be disrespectful."

She headed for the shop. "Do you want me to start on the website orders?" she asked over her shoulder.

"Please," I said, struggling to keep a neutral expression on my face.

Liz shook her head. "Don't you dare smile," she said, shaking one perfectly manicured finger at me, the color, Cherry Baby, unless I was mistaken. "You're encouraging her."

I remembered Stella saying I was spit out of Gram's mouth and I realized the same could be said for Avery and Liz. "Always glad to help," I said with grin.

Liz shook her head. She looked elegant as always in a navy wool duffel coat with wooden toggle buttons, dark gray wool trousers and heeled gray boots. I tried to imagine Liz in a pair of Bean boots and smiled at the image.

Charlotte came in, tying the strings of her yellow apron. Even in flat shoes she was a bit taller than me, and unlike me, she never slouched. She and Nick had the same warm smile and the same kind brown eyes that could darken in a flash if either one of them was angered.

"Rose says Vincent Swift is dead," she said.

I nodded. "Stella was here."

Charlotte glanced at Liz. "Well, I'm not going to pretend I'm sorry," Liz said. "He wasn't a quality person."

Rose had quietly joined us. Liz fixed her attention on her friend. "You want to help her find his killer, don't you?"

Rose nodded. "I do. I think Stella has been put in an untenable position. And no matter how unpleasant a man Vincent Swift was, he didn't deserve to die the way he did. 'Nothing to look backward to with pride, And nothing to look forward to with hope,'" She quoted Robert Frost's "Death of the Hired Man" in a quiet voice.

Liz turned to look at me. "What do you want to do?" she asked.

"I want to find out who killed the man," I said.

"All right, I'm in," Liz said with an offhand shrug.

Rose stared at her in surprise. "You are?"

She nodded. "Yes. Stella is good people and you, Rose Jackson, are right. No matter how unpleasant Vincent Swift was, he didn't deserve to pretty much die in the street like that." She reached over and gently tapped the underside of my chin with her hand. "Close your mouth, missy," she said. "There are flies around even in the middle of winter." She patted my cheek a little more vigorously than was necessary and headed for the back door. "Toodles," she said, waving her gloves over her shoulder. "I have places to go and people to see."

Rose shook her head. "After all the years I've known that woman, she can still surprise me."

"Toodles?" I muttered, mostly to myself. I'd forgotten that Rose had, as she explained it, "ears like a wolf."

"A shortened version of 'toodaloo,'" she said, "which is likely a mangled version of the French phrase, 'à tout à l'heure,' which translates, approximately to 'See you later.'"

Charlotte was having difficulty not smiling.

"Umm, good to know, thank you," I said.

Rose turned her attention to Charlotte. "And you're in?" she asked.

"Absolutely," Charlotte said. "Look how Stella stepped up for Ellie when she needed help. Now we step up for her."

Rose nodded with satisfaction. Then she turned and headed back to the sun porch.

"So it's official? We have a case?" I said to her retreating back.

She didn't miss a step. "We have a case," she said.

Chapter 6

I left Charlotte dusting the shop and went upstairs to my office. Elvis was sprawled in the middle of my desk, one paw poking the air as though he were using an invisible tablet. I dropped onto my chair. He rolled onto his side and I reached over to stroke his fur. "Stella is the Angels' new client," I said.

"Mrrr," he said, nuzzling my hand. He didn't seem surprised.

"And I need to call Nick." I wasn't sure how he was going to react to Rose and crew taking on Stella as a client. Nick and Rose had banged heads before over the Angels' cases, although lately Rose had been referring to him as "part of the team."

Elvis looked at me and then looked at my cell phone lying on the table by his back feet.

"I don't have to call him this minute."

His green eyes were fixed on my face. He didn't blink. He didn't so much as twitch a whisker.

"Stop staring at me," I said. "It's creepy."

That didn't stop him. It was a cat thing.

I reached for the phone. "Fine. Look, I'm calling him." I swear the cat was smiling.

"Hey, Sarah, what's up?" Nick said when he answered.

"I wanted to let you know that Rose and the others have a case."

"Stella."

"Yes."

"It doesn't surprise me. They've all known her for a long time.

"Nick, you know she wouldn't kill anyone," I said.

For a moment Nick didn't say anything. Then I heard him sigh softly. "Do I have to give you my speech?"

"Would that be the 'Popcorn makes a perfectly good supper' speech or the 'Under the right circumstances anyone could be a killer' speech?"

"The second one," he said. "Although the first one is also true, as you well know." He was in a good mood.

I leaned back in my chair and Elvis jumped down into my lap. "It was the injury to his head that killed Swift, wasn't it?" I said.

"We shouldn't be discussing this."

"Oh, c'mon," I said. "I saw the man's head. I saw the blood."

Silence stretched between us and I pressed my lips together so I wouldn't be the first one to end it. Elvis nuzzled my hand and I started stroking his fur again.

"Yes," Nick finally said.

"That glass ball."

He made a sound of exasperation. "I didn't say that and I'm *not* saying it."

"I'm not saying you are," I said. "But I was there and I saw the blood on it." I didn't say that I'd also seen blood on Stella's hands. "I knelt in the snow and held Vincent Swift's hand and urged him to hold on."

My voice had gotten louder and I was surprised by how emotional I suddenly felt.

"That was really kind," Nick said, "which doesn't surprise me, because that's the type of person you are."

"I'm not so sure about that," I said. I hadn't done anything that anyone else who had walked around that corner wouldn't have done.

"Well, I am," he said. "And for the record, I'm really glad that you and Jess are okay. And Stella, for that matter. If the two of you or her had walked around that corner a little sooner . . ." He didn't finish the thought. I heard him clear his throat. "You're the one who wants to find Swift's killer, aren't you?"

"We all agreed to take the case," I hedged.

"But you want to clear Stella."

Elvis seemed to have gotten bored with hearing only half of the conversation. He jumped down with a low "mrrr" and headed out, probably downstairs to see what was going on in the store.

"I'm not saying I don't have faith in you or in Michelle," I said. "It's just that Gram and Stella have been friends since they were playing Red Rover on the playground. And I know I sound like a broken record but—"

"—I know," Nick said before I could finish the sentence. "You don't want anyone to think Stella could have killed someone. I don't want that, either. I don't have an agenda. My job is just to gather information and look at the evidence."

I shifted in the chair and propped my feet up on the corner of the desk. "But you can't help having an opinion about who did what to whom. Was it Professor Plum in the library with the candlestick or was it Miss Scarlet?"

To my surprise he laughed.

"What's so funny?" I asked.

"I'm starting to regret ever unearthing that game from my mother's garage and playing it with you," he said.

Now it was my turn to laugh. "No, no, no," I said. "I'm blameless when it comes to Clue. You dug out that game because you wanted to show Josh Evans's cousin how smart you were. She was visiting that one summer. Come to think of it, I'm not sure she ever came back for another visit."

"She moved to California with her mother after her parents got divorced," Nick said.

"And you know that how?"

He laughed again. "How do you think? I asked Josh. She was really cute. And you're doing a Rose on me."

I frowned even though he couldn't see me. "What is 'doing a Rose'?"

"Driving the subject in a completely different direction."

"I am not," I began indignantly. Then I stopped. "Okay, so maybe I was, but I swear it wasn't on purpose."

"I'm just going to say one thing and then I need to go," Nick said.

"What is it?' I said.

"Like I said, I try not to make judgments, but you know that when people are angry or upset, sometimes, in the moment, they do things they normally wouldn't even think of doing. You also know I don't believe people just snap like some kind of overstretched rubber band, but sometimes they do get pushed beyond their limit."

I opened my mouth to tell him that wasn't Stella, but he somehow seemed to know what I'd been about to say. "That being said, my mother has also known Stella for a very long time, and Charlotte McPhee Elliot is a pretty good judge of character."

"Yes, she is," I said.

"I really need to go," Nick said. "Is it okay if I stop by later? I just have a few questions for you."

"I'll be here."

After we said good-bye, I tried Josh's office. His assistant explained that he was in court all day. "He said to tell you that he does want to talk to you," she said.

I gave her my cell number even though I was pretty sure he had it. Then I ended the call, put the phone on vibrate and tucked it in my pocket before I went back downstairs.

Charlotte was with a customer looking at a 1960s vintage walnut finish cabinet with four pull-out drawers on one side and a hinged door on the other. The Danish design was sleek, without embellishment; all it had needed when we found it was to be cleaned up and the legs replaced. Given how closely the woman was examining the piece, I suspected we'd have a sale.

Avery was in the workshop carefully packing a retro wall clock to mail to a customer. Elvis was sitting on the work bench, "helping." The clock didn't work but the purchaser didn't care. He was more interested in the design: black cats on a stylized blue background. As usual, Avery had a stack of bracelets sliding along her arm and it made me smile to see she was wearing the bracelet with the cat charm I'd given her back in the fall.

She pushed her hair back off her face and glanced at me. "We're getting low on bubble wrap."

"That's not a problem," I said. "Jess has a bunch of it down at her shop. She's been saving it anytime they get parcels. She has some boxes, too."

"So we're recycling," Avery said, adding a bit more tissue paper over the clock's face.

"As much as we can," I said. "We're reusing boxes and bubble wrap and paper. And you could argue the whole store is one big recycling project."

"Could we start worm recycling?"

I was lost. "How do you recycle worms?" I asked.

Avery and Elvis exchanged a look. I could almost swear the cat rolled his eyes.

"It's a way of composting, using worms," Avery said, head still bent over the package.

"Is it smelly?"

She finally looked up at me. "I don't know."

"So find out," I said. "Do some research and when you have the facts get back to me."

She eyed me with more than a little skepticism in her gaze. "And you'll really do it?"

"I'll consider it. Get me the details."

"I will." Then she looked at Elvis, held up her hand and said, "High five."

To my surprise he put a paw to her hand.

Avery smiled at him, then turned back to me "Hey, Sarah, what's my budget for the window display for Valentine's Day?" Avery's front window designs got more attention than anything I ever came up with. People still talked about her Valentine's display with mannequins for the band KISS.

"Keep it under a hundred dollars," I said. She'd never spent that much on supplies for one of her designs.

She nodded thoughtfully. "Okay. Can I use anything here in the workroom or from out in the old garage?"

"As long as nothing gets damaged, yes."

"Can I trade something from the shop for things I might need?" she asked.

"That depends." Now I was starting to wonder exactly what she had in mind for the display. "Ask me or Mac first."

Elvis nudged her hand with his head and she began to absently stroke his fur. "And can I do whatever I want in the window—I mean design-wise?"

This was going to be an interesting Valentine's display. "You can," I said. Then I held up a finger. "The usual rules apply."

"Nothing mean, nothing obscene."

I nodded. "Otherwise have fun." I had no doubt she would.

Both Rose and Mr. P. were in their office. My brother, Liam, with help from Nick, had done an outstanding job turning the sunporch into working space for the Angels. They had replaced the old, drafty windows with new ones and added thermal shades to keep the heat out during the summer and in during the winter. Liam had laid a durable vinyl plank floor and installed a baseboard electric heater for the coldest months. The walls were painted a pale, off white color and there was lots of insulation behind the new drywall.

There was a chalkboard on the wall above Mr. P.'s desk, flanked by a couple of wall sconces that Rose had chosen. To the right of the desk, Mr. P. had placed an easel that held an oversized pad of paper. It was perfect for working out a timeline or keeping a list of what needed to be done next. The big farm-style table we used for meetings (aka tea and cake) was at the far end of the room, surrounded by a collection of ever-changing mismatched chairs from the shop.

Liam had managed to keep the renovations within my very limited budget. Gram held the mortgage on the shop, and as far as she was concerned I could take the next thirty years to pay it off, but I wanted to retire the debt a lot sooner than that.

Mr. P. smiled when he caught sight of me. He was a little bald man with a few gray tufts of hair that stuck straight out from his head most of the time and kind eyes behind his wire-framed glasses. He was wearing a brown-and-green plaid flannel shirt with a brown cardigan sweater and he smelled like peppermints.

"How did the hearing test go?" I asked.

"For now all my original parts are in good condition."

I smiled. "I'm glad to hear it."

"Do you by any chance have any news to share?" Rose asked. She tipped her head to one side. In her bright scarlet sweater she reminded me of a tiny bird.

"Yes, I do," I said. "Josh is in court all day but I did talk to Nick."

"Did you learn anything that might help us?" Mr. P. asked.

"He did tell me that Vincent Swift died from that head wound I saw."

Mr. P. nodded. "That's what I expected to hear but it's good to have confirmation. Rosie said Stella was holding a glass sphere. Am I correct that it was the murder weapon?"

I brushed a stray strand of hair off my cheek. "I couldn't get Nick to say so but I think it's a safe assumption. I wish it wasn't. Stella's fingerprints are all over that glass ball. That doesn't look good for her."

Mr. P. took off his glasses and removed the little cloth he used for cleaning them from his pocket. It was something I'd noticed him do from time to time when he was working something out. "It's not necessarily bad, Sarah," he said as he began to polish the left lens.

"What do you mean?"

"Wouldn't a guilty person have tried to get rid of the murder weapon? Stuff it inside their coat or at least throw it away? Stella was holding on to it, which to my way of thinking suggests she hadn't done anything wrong."

"That makes sense," I said. "Although I'm not sure the police will see it that way."

"Michelle is a very smart young woman," Rose said. "She won't jump to any conclusions."

Mr. P. put his glasses back on, refolded the little square of cloth and tucked it back in his pocket. "Sarah, would you mind going over what happened last night one more time? You must be sick of telling the story but I would like to hear it firsthand."

"I don't mind," I said, perching on the corner of his desk. I went through the details again, tracing the path Jess and I had walked from The Black Bear to the corner where we'd turned and discovered Stella and Vincent Swift, trying to be as accurate as possible.

Mr. P. saved his questions until I'd finished.

"Were there a lot of people at the pub?" he asked.

I shook my head. "It wasn't even half full," I said. "Mondays are pretty quiet."

"What about the boardwalk? Did you see many people?"

I linked my fingers together and rested my hands on the top of my head. "No. Six, eight, maybe. And they were all headed in the opposite direction."

He asked if the streetlights were working. (They were.) How far were Stella and Swift from the corner? (Maybe twenty-five feet.) How cold was it? (Certainly below freezing.)

"Did you see anyone walking ahead of you?"

I slid my hands down over the back of my head and stared into space, searching my memory. Rose put a hand on Mr. P.'s shoulder for a moment and then slipped out. "I didn't see anyone in front of us." I said.

"Did you hear any footsteps?" he asked.

I remembered the sharp sound of Jess's boots as we walked—they had heels—but not of anyone else walking. I shook my head. "No."

"Did you see Rose leave this room?" he asked.

I hadn't expected that question. "I did," I said. "You had just asked me if I remembered seeing anyone walking ahead of Jess and me." I smiled, feeling pleased that I'd passed Mr. P.'s little test of my recall.

He smiled back at me. "And when did Rose come back?"

A trick question. "She didn't."

"Yes, I did."

Rose's voice came from over my shoulder. Confused, I turned around. She was less than three feet behind me. "How did I not hear you?" I said. I shifted back around to stare at Mr. P. "How could I not know Rose was behind me?"

Rose came to stand next to me. She put a hand on my shoulder. "You were focused on answering Alfred's questions and trying to remember what happened last night. I wanted you to see that you won't remember everything perfectly. You can't. Our brains don't work that way. And that's all right."

I rubbed the space between my eyebrows with two fingers. "But I could have missed something last night—someone running away, a car starting, some piece of evidence I didn't even know was important."

"It's possible," Mr. P. said. "Memory is fallible. It's not a perfect freeze-frame of what happened. Think of it as a kind of reenactment of what occurred, filtered through your mind."

"That doesn't sound very reliable."

"Sometimes it isn't." He picked up his pen and pointed it at me like a gun. "Johnson and Scott studied what's known as the Weapon Effect. Basically what they discovered was if there was a weapon present, the witnesses' attention was focused on that weapon and they remembered fewer other details of what happened." He set the pen down again. "In your case, you were in an intense and emotional situation and all of your focus would have been on Mr. Swift and Stella. I'm not saying you missed anything, just that you might have. I'll talk to Jess. She may have noticed different details than you did."

When I walked back into the shop I discovered that—no surprise—Charlotte had sold the cabinet. "Mac's loading it into the customer's SUV," she said. "And I have a feeling she's going to be back for a couple of those Pyrex casserole dishes. She looked at them three times."

Mac came back inside. He hadn't put on a coat and his cheeks were flushed with color.

"Thank you," Charlotte said. "I'm not sure Avery and I could have gotten that cabinet into that woman's vehicle."

Mac came across the floor and stood in front of her, flexing his right arm. "I'm very strong. Wanna feel my muscle?" he asked, waggling his eyebrows.

Charlotte looked at me. "Did that line work on you?"

I hung my head in mock shame. "Yes, it did."

She reached over and patted Mac's arm. "Lucky for you," she said.

Mac laughed.

Charlotte looked around the room. "So what are we bringing in to fill that empty space?"

"What about that small cabinet?" I said.

Mac made a face. "I'm still not happy with the drawer pulls."

I knew that sometimes the small details like drawer pulls or doorknobs were what caught a customer's eye. "Okay. We could bring in that wicker chair and ottoman or the rocking chair."

"The rocking chair," Charlotte immediately said. "This is curl-up-with-a-good-book weather, not lounge-in-the-sunporch weather. The rocking chair will sell faster."

I pictured the big wooden chair sitting in the empty place on the floor. "You're right." I said. "You could dress it with the last two pillows from Jess, and there's a blue blanket under the stairs that Rose knit. We had it draped over the back of the wing chair that Avery sold on the weekend."

"What if someone wants to buy the blanket?"

"Sell it," I said. "Rose gave me the okay. Everything in the shop is for sale."

Charlotte gave me a sly side-eye. "Everything?"

I nodded. "Everything."

"Even Mac's muscles?" she teased.

I laughed. "No, not Mac's muscles." He gave us a smug smile and flexed again. "But they are for rent," I added.

Rose and Mr. P. spent the afternoon in the Angels' office, working on the case, I assumed. Mac brought in the rocking chair. Then he found three matte black drawer handles, changed out the ones he didn't like on the small cabinet and brought that in, too.

After a lot of back-and-forth, I had painted the cabinet a warm tan shade, except for the top, which had been sanded, stained a toasty honey color and varnished. I had a feeling the piece wouldn't last long in the shop.

Charlotte got the last two pillows Jess had made from the storage space under the stairs and put them on the seat of the rocking chair. Jess had used pieces from several quilts too worn to save to make the pillows. Charlotte also added the teal blue blanket Rose had made. She set a small teddy bear on the seat as well. Avery had insisted the bear could not be left at a summer flea market we'd gone to. It had looked a little forlorn sitting at the end of a long table. Rose had knit a vest for the bear and I thought it looked quite dapper.

"Sarah, may I move some of those casserole dishes to the top of the cabinet and add a couple of other decorative items?" Charlotte asked. She and Avery were eyeing the piece of furniture, both of them with their arms crossed over their midsections.

"Do whatever you think will work," I said as I headed for the stairs.

I changed into an old shirt and jeans that I kept in my office for painting and other dirty work. I had decided to use the leftover tan paint from the cabinet for the two chairs I hadn't been able to settle on a color for.

I was washing my brushes at the end of the day when Rose came in from outside. She stomped the snow off of her boots and joined me. "How about coming for dessert after supper, sweetie?" she said. "I took some stewed rhubarb out of the freezer and I'm making biscuits and custard sauce."

The rhubarb had come from our backyard. Rose and Charlotte and I had chopped and cooked piles of it back in the spring. I'd already eaten all the containers from my freezer. "That sounds wonderful," I said.

"Splendid," Rose said. "We can talk about what we need to do next." I knew she was referring to the case. "Have you made any plans for Valentine's Day?"

Conversational detour. "Umm . . . yes," I said. My right sleeve was sliding down. I held my arm out over the sink and Rose rolled the sleeve up again. "Avery is doing the window, though I have no idea what it will look like."

Rose shook her head. "No. I mean for Mac."

"Well, I haven't finalized anything."

She gave me a pitying smile. "So, no."

"Okay, no." I felt embarrassed since I knew both she and Mr. P. had made plans. I turned off the water and shook the brushes in the sink.

Rose took a step backward before the water starting flying. "You know, dear, there's nothing wrong with the traditional approach: a nice meal, a little wine, a slow dancing, a little chocolate for dessert."

"Or maybe we'll go out."

"Sweetie, you need to decide. You can't wait until the last minute or you won't get a reservation at a decent time. You don't want to be eating a romantic dinner with the Shady Pines crowd."

Shady Pines was the name Rose had given to Legacy Place, the seniors' apartment complex she'd lived in before she'd taken the apartment in my house. The nickname wasn't meant to be a compliment.

I nodded, but I was thinking that I wanted something different. I just didn't know what.

As though she could read my mind Rose said, "Or you could both get matching tattoos. They can be small and not in a place everyone can see." She gave me what could only be described as a naughty smile and one eyebrow went up, while I hoped an earthquake would hit Maine at that very moment, opening a large crevice underneath my feet that I could fall into. I could feel my cheeks burning. Did this mean Rose and Mr. P. had matching tattoos? I did not need to know that.

Luckily there was no more talk of body adornment on the drive home. "What time do you want me?" I said to Rose as we pulled into the driveway.

"Just come when you're ready," she said.

My house was an 1860s Victorian that had been divided into three apartments almost forty years ago now. It had been let go when I bought it. The paint was peeling on the outside and the colors were garish on the inside, but I could see that it had good bones. My dad and Liam had spent a lot of weekends helping me fix up my main-floor apartment and Gram's second-floor one. Rose's small unit at the back of the house had been the last one to be finished. Her need to have somewhere to live after Legacy Place terminated their "arrangement" was what had finally pushed me to get the last few things done.

After supper I headed down to Rose's apartment in my fuzzy slippers. Mac was playing hockey with

Cleveland and some of his friends. Not only did I buy from Cleveland pretty regularly for the shop, he and his brother had helped with security on one of the Angels' cases.

Gram was sitting at Rose's kitchen table. "I didn't know you'd be here," I said, leaning down to wrap her in a hug.

"Rose said she needed to pick my brain," Gram said. "And she might have mentioned biscuits."

"She used rhubarb to bribe me," I said.

"The word you're looking for is 'incentivize,' not 'bribe,'" Rose retorted. She was getting a large bowl from the refrigerator. I went to help her.

"Thank you," she said. "You can just set it on the counter."

"Gram, where's John?" I asked over my shoulder. I looked at Rose. "Teacups?"

She nodded.

"He's playing hockey," Gram said. She smiled at Mr. P., who set the sugar bowl and a pitcher of milk in the middle of the table.

I turned to look at her. "Hang on, with Cleveland and his friends?"

She nodded. "He was a goalie in college."

I assumed she meant John. "Mac's playing as well," I said. "He said they were short of players."

"They needed a goalie," Gram said. "John said he hadn't played in years. Cleveland said it was him or someone who hadn't been in goal ever."

"That would have been me," Mr. P. said.

"You play hockey?" I said. He was full of surprises.

He nodded. "I used to. I haven't played competitively in years and I was a forward, never a goalie, but I do know a lot about the position, in theory."

"Well, I'm sorry John took away your chance to play tonight," Gram said, sending me an *Am I missing something?* look.

"Oh, don't worry about that," Mr. P. said. "Since he's actually played the position he was a much better choice."

I arranged four teacups on the counter.

"We're going to need more than that, sweetie," Rose said as she took a pan of biscuits out of the oven. They smelled wonderful.

I saw Gram eye the biscuits as Rose moved them to a wire rack. "Well, John can be a little competitive at times," she said. "I reminded him this was just for fun and the final score doesn't matter."

A voice from the doorway said, "Of course the score matters. If it didn't, then why would anyone keep score?"

Gram laughed and shook her head.

Liz, who was standing in the doorway, said, "Shake your head at me all you want. It doesn't make it any less true."

The kettle boiled and I made the tea while Rose finished putting the biscuits on the rack and Mr. P. took Liz's coat.

I got another cup from the cupboard. "I didn't realize this was a case meeting," I said.

Rose looked surprised. "I'm sorry," she said. "I thought that was obvious."

"We usually have our meetings at the shop."

Rose gestured at the large container of rhubarb. "My dish would never fit in that little tiny fridge."

"But Nick's not here," I said jokingly.

At that exact moment there was a knock at the door. Mr. P. opened it and Nick was standing there.

Rose just smiled.

Chapter 7

Nick let Mr. P. take his jacket. He bent down to give Charlotte a kiss and said hello to Gram and Liz before coming to help me put everything on the table. He made a shooing motion at Rose when she tried to carry the dish of custard. He was well over six feet and he seemed to take up all the space in Rose's small kitchen. Nick wasn't quite the wannabe musician I'd hung out with all those summers I'd spent in North Harbor growing up. But he still had the same disheveled sandy hair and warm brown eyes that I'd crushed on when I was fifteen.

"I somehow missed that this was a team meeting," he said to me in a low voice.

"You and me both," I said. I bumped him with my hip as I reached for a plate for the biscuits. "Buck up, dude. There's custard, and I think we might be learning a team cheer tonight."

He made a face at me.

"Do you want a cup of tea?" I asked once I'd made sure everyone else had a cup.

"Why not?" he said.

I poured a cup for each of us and handed his to him. We leaned against the counter, side by side.

"I forgot to get the folding chairs," Rose said, starting to get to her feet.

"We're fine," Nick said. "Sit."

Rose looked at me.

"Nick's right," I said. "We're fine. And these biscuits are delicious."

She smiled. "Thank you. Alfred helped me make them."

Nick gave the old man a thumbs-up. His mouth was too full to talk.

"Did you talk to Jess?" I asked, keeping my voice low because Rose really did have ears like a wolf.

He licked a dab of custard off his spoon before answering. "I did. I'm sorry I didn't make it over to see you. Another case got in the way. Can we find a few minutes to talk later?"

I took a sip from my tea and then set the cup down on the counter. "Sure. I didn't hear from Michelle, either."

"That's probably because she had to testify in court—some last-minute change in the order of witnesses. She'll probably call you tomorrow."

Rose clapped her hands then and we all automatically looked at her. "You all know that Stella has asked us to investigate the death of Vincent Swift last night and we have accepted the case. What we need to do now is come up with a plan. Since Sarah was there, we know that Mr. Swift died from being hit over the head with a glass sphere."

"Technically the police haven't confirmed that yet," Nick said.

"That's true. Thank you, Nicolas," Rose said. "We *believe* Mr. Swift was killed by several blows to the head with a glass sphere, which we do know they will find Stella's fingerprints on because both Sarah and Jess saw her holding it." She looked at Nick and he gave a small nod.

"This doesn't appear to be a premeditated crime," Rose continued, "but we need to look at who had issues with the man, since it's likely the killer is someone he knew and not a stranger."

Liz gave a snort of derision. "That's going to be a long list."

Gram was already nodding her head. "I'm sorry but Liz is right. Vincent alienated a lot of people over the years. I can think of two or three off the top of my head."

"We're probably thinking of the same people," Liz said.

Rose smiled. "That works out perfectly. The two of you can make the list." She turned to Charlotte. "What do you know about his family?"

Charlotte set down her spoon. "Vincent is—was—a distant cousin to Daniel Swift." Daniel Swift's branch of the family tree owned a lot of property in and around North Harbor. "They're both descendants of the originals Swifts who settled this area. Clayton McNamara will know all the family connections. I'll call him and put together a family tree."

"Yes, I think it would help," Rose said. "Thank you."

"I can tell you that Vincent only had one child," Charlotte said. "A son. He doesn't live here in North Harbor."

"Do you know the young man's name?" Mr. P. asked.

Charlotte looked at Liz. "Walker? Or is it Wyatt?"

Liz frowned. "Neither one of those is right." She thought for a moment. "It's William," she said. "After Vincent's great-grandfather, I think."

Charlotte nodded as she added milk to her tea. "You're right. It is William."

"I'll see if I can find him," Mr. P. said.

"What about the accident?" I said, scraping my spoon around the side of my bowl, which was somehow empty.

"I don't see how that has anything to do with this," Nick immediately said.

"Wait a minute. What accident are you talking about?" Gram asked. She looked from Nick to me.

I glanced at Rose. "Go ahead, dear," she said.

I set my empty dish on the counter. "It happened while you and John were on your extended honeymoon," I said. "Vincent Swift had been at a meeting at the high school. It was when they were thinking about renovating the gym and the locker rooms. His godson, Jacob, was also there to meet his girlfriend, Madison, who had volleyball practice. The kids were planning to walk home—neither one of them had a car—but it was cold and starting to snow and Swift offered them a ride. Jacob had only had his driver's license for a few months and he was always looking for the chance to get behind the wheel. Swift let him drive his SUV."

I took a breath and let it out. "The car went off the road . . . and Madison was killed."

"Oh no," Gram said softly.

"Swift had a concussion and a broken collarbone. Jacob sustained a serious head injury and neither one of them could remember anything about the accident. Everything after getting to the volleyball game was a blank."

"Jacob was charged with criminally negligent homicide," Nick said. "Mr. Swift paid for a very good lawyer, who was able to negotiate a deal that saw Jacob spend just nine months in jail and do some community service. He also lost his license for two years."

"That's horribly sad," Gram said, "but it would be a motive for someone to hurt the young man, not Vincent."

Across the table Mr. P. was nodding. "That's true, Isabel, but Mr. Swift insisted the stretch of road where the accident had taken place had not been properly salted and sanded. He sued. The road crew had stopped for a coffee break—which they were entitled to—but Swift's lawyer was able to show the crew lingered longer than their allotted time. The salt truck driver and his supervisor ultimately lost their jobs, and there were a lot of hard feelings in town over that."

"The whole thing was a mess," Nick said, folding his arms over his chest. "It wasn't as though the crew spent a lot of extra time on their break, plus there were questions as to whether the kid had been speeding. Because both he and Swift had head injuries that left them with no memory of the accident, it was hard to determine exactly what happened."

"What about the lawsuit?" Gram asked.

"The state lost," Liz said. She lifted the teapot as if trying to judge whether there was any tea left and then poured herself another cup. "They struck a deal to pay a smaller amount of money immediately instead of it being tied up for years on appeal. I have it on good authority that both Vincent and the young man received high six-figure settlements."

Gram leaned forward to look at her. "What about the girl's family?"

"They weren't part of the lawsuit," Nick said.

I looked at Rose. "I could see what I can dig up just in case there's a connection somehow."

She nodded. "I think that's a good idea." She looked around the room. "We're looking into Vincent Swift himself, his possible enemies and that past lawsuit. Are we missing anything at this point?"

"What about the library?" Charlotte asked. "That's where Stella was coming from. Maybe the killer came from there, too."

"Good point," Rose said. "The library is a busy spot in the winter months—lots of groups meet there." She smiled. "And I think I have a couple of books that are due."

"What about Stella?" Nick said.

I turned to look at him, narrowing my eyes. "What do you mean?" I said.

"Maybe someone saw her walking. Some of the

businesses along the waterfront have security cameras. I know the hotel does, although that's probably too far away to do any good."

Mr. P. tipped his head to one side, a thoughtful expression in his blue eyes. "I'll see what I can find," he said. "Thank you for the suggestion."

Liz tapped the side of her cup with her spoon. We all turned to look at her. "Where did that glass ball come from?" she said.

"I'm sorry, Elizabeth, what do you mean?" Mr. P. said.

"Where did the glass sphere that Vincent was hit with come from? The one Stella picked up. Did he have it with him or did the killer? It's not the sort of thing you generally carry in your pocket."

Mr. P. was nodding before Liz finished talking. "You're right," he said. "That is important. I'm on it." He looked over at me. "Sarah, would you map out the route you and Jess took, from the pub to where you discovered Stella and Mr. Swift?"

I nodded. "I will."

"Is that it, then?" Rose asked. No one said anything. "Splendid! Now, who wants more tea and seconds on dessert?"

Nick had already filled the kettle and put it on to boil. Other detective agencies depended on technology or connections in law enforcement. This one depended on tea.

Nick leaned against the counter next to me again and I nudged him with my shoulder. "You know you want seconds," I said.

He gave me a cocky smile and patted his midsection with one hand. "It takes a lot of energy to keep this well-oiled, magnificent machine running at peak efficiency, you know."

I sputtered with laughter. "You are so full of it."

He pushed himself upright again. "So does that mean you're not having seconds?" he asked.

I waffled between how good Rose's biscuits tasted and how cold it would be going for a run in the morning. "Well, I wouldn't want you to have to refuel that 'magnificent machine' all by yourself," I said.

Nick got us seconds while I helped Rose make a fresh pot of tea. Then we ate and talked about what had been going on in both our lives. "I talked to Liam a couple of days ago," Nick said around a mouthful of biscuit and custard.

"So did I," I said. "I'm still trying to convince him that he should move to North Harbor full-time."

"Don't tell him I told you this, but you might be wearing him down. He's thinking about taking fewer projects this fall and maybe just spending some time around here."

"He didn't tell me that."

Nick shrugged. "He's your brother. He's not going to let you get the idea that you have any influence on what he does."

"Hold still," I said. I reached over and wiped a smear of custard from his chin. "So how did you get to be such an expert on sibling relationships?" I asked. "You're an only child."

"Watching the two of you," he said with a smirk. He craned his neck to look in my bowl.

I put one hand over the top. "Don't even think

about it. I will jam this spoon right up the nose of your 'magnificent machine.'"

Nick laughed. "I'm assuming you and Jess will be at the jam on Thursday," he said.

"I will be," I said, licking a bit of fruit from my thumb and hoping no one noticed.

"Assuming Rose doesn't solve the case in the next two days and you don't have to go along while she makes a citizen's arrest."

I jabbed my spoon in the air. "You jest, but that could happen. Don't underestimate them."

Nick swiped a hand over his mouth. "I learned that one the hard way."

I started to laugh.

"It's not funny," he said, glaring at me.

"Oh yes it is," I said. "I can still see you, all righteous indignation, explaining how they couldn't take any more cases because the state requires private investigators to be licensed. And then Mr. P. quoted the relevant statute word for word because he'd met all the requirements and he'd already gotten his license." I pressed my lips together but I couldn't stop laughing. Nick had thought he'd done an end run around them but they had in fact outsmarted him. To his credit he had (eventually) been a gracious loser.

Nick made a face at me. "I'm changing the subject," he said. "Where's Mac?"

"Playing hockey."

He frowned. "Where?"

"With Cleveland and some of his friends. They were short a couple of guys. It's just for fun."

It was Nick's turn to laugh. "If your idea of fun is crushing your opponent, sure."

"Oh crap," I said. "John is playing as well. He's their goalie for the night. Although Gram did say he is kind of competitive."

"I can't wait to hear the recap after the game," Nick said.

I slugged his arm.

His expression turned serious. "So tell me what happened last night."

I repeated the story for what felt like the hundredth time. Nick asked me to describe exactly how Swift had been lying, what I had done, what I'd touched. He wanted to know what I'd noticed about the head wound and about Swift's hands. I tried to picture the street as I answered each question and I tried to remember them all, thinking these might be things Mr. P. would want to know as well.

Finally Nick ran out of things to ask me. "I should get going," he said.

"You're not staying around to learn the team cheer?" I teased.

He shook his head. "Seriously, try to stay out of trouble, and keep this bunch out of trouble as well."

"Nothing's going to go wrong," I said.

"I hope you're right," he said.

I smiled. "I am." Still I slid one hand behind my back and tapped gently three times on the wooden cupboard behind me.

Just in case.

Chapter 8

Nick hugged Rose and dropped a kiss on the top of his mother's head. He stopped to say something to Mr. P., who had gotten Nick's coat. Then he was gone.

Once Nick had left, Gram got up and started to clear the table. I went over to her, making a shooing motion with one hand.

She looked at me and smiled. "Are you trying to herd the chickens, my darling girl?" she asked.

"I'm trying to herd you," I said. "Sit. I'll get these things."

"Has anyone ever told you that you can be a little bossy?"

"Let me see," I said. There's you, Mom, Rose, Liz, Charlotte, Liam, my fourth-grade teacher." I ticked off the names on my fingers.

Gram laughed. "I have no idea where you could have picked up that kind of behavior."

"Me either," I said with an almost completely straight face.

"Thank you for helping Stella," she said. "Last night and now. We go back a long way, and I know she has a good heart."

"She's a good person." I seemed to be saying that a lot, but it was true. "Look how she stepped up for Ellie and the kids."

"How is Ellie?" Gram asked. "Have you heard from her lately?"

"She's doing really well. All the kids are in school now and Ellie is teaching kindergarten."

She smiled. "I'm glad that things worked out for her. First thing in the morning I'll start making a list of the different groups Vincent has been involved with in the past several years. He did tend to rub people the wrong way. And if there's anything else I can do to help, let me know."

"Thanks," I said, wrapping her in a hug. She smelled liked vanilla.

"Come and have supper with us soon. And bring Elvis."

"I will," I promised.

Gram went to say good night to Rose and Mr. P. and I finished clearing the table. I saw Liz raise an eyebrow at Charlotte, who nodded in return. "We're going to hit the road," Liz said. She looked at me. "I'll talk to Channing. I'll be surprised if he doesn't know some dirt about Vincent." She held up a finger. "And not a word about my love life."

I pantomimed zipping my lips.

Channing was Channing Caulfield, a former bank manager and financial planner who over the years had often advised Liz on matters related to her family's charitable foundation. Liz had recently taken over running the foundation again from her brother and Channing had been helping. He'd also been carrying a torch for Liz for decades, as Charlotte—who had gone to school with Channing and called him Chuckie— liked to say. I just liked to tease Liz about him, a little payback for all the meddling she'd done in my romantic life.

"Do you think there was someone in Vincent Swift's personal life who could have killed him?" I asked.

Liz wrapped a soft gray scarf around her neck. "I know what they say about not speaking ill of the dead," she said. "But he was a totally self-absorbed person, and that kind of person does make enemies. I wish I could say differently but I can't." She slipped on her jacket. "I didn't like the man and I don't think there are many people who will truly grieve his loss." She looked sad. "That's not much of a legacy. Especially when you have more miles on the road behind you than you do on the road ahead."

I threw my arms around her. "That will never be you. Avery loves you, I love you and so do lots of other people."

Her eyes were suddenly and suspiciously bright. "I love you, too," she said. "Even though you can be very saucy."

I put a hand to my chest. "Me? Saucy? I think you've mixed me up with someone else."

Liz shook her head and pulled her gloves out of the

pocket of her duffle coat. "Let's roll," she said to Charlotte.

Charlotte smiled and gave my arm a squeeze as she passed me. "I'll see you tomorrow," she said.

"Tell Uncle Channing hello," I called after Liz.

"Saucy," she retorted without looking back.

I carried the dishes over to the kitchen and started loading the dishwasher. "I can do that," Mr. P. protested.

"I know you can," I said. "But I was thinking I could keep my hands busy while I tell you what Nick asked me."

"Did you get anything out of him?" Rose asked. She was rearranging the chairs and Mr. P. went to help her.

I shook my head as I put all the spoons in the cutlery rack. "Nothing. But I can tell you he mostly wanted to know about Vincent Swift's body—how he was lying, what I noticed about his hands and the injury to the back of his head."

"That makes sense," Mr. P. said. "Nicolas does work for the medical examiner. It's the sort of evidence he's trained to look for."

I looked over at him. "Do you think there's any way that what happened could have been an accident?"

"Do you?" he said.

I sighed. "No. There was no ice on the sidewalk, just a few scattered patches of snow. No broken pavement. No potholes. There was nothing that looked like he'd lost his footing. Stella, Jess and I all walked on the same stretch of sidewalk and none of us had any problem. Except for the head wound, there were no other injuries to Swift's body. He wasn't cut or scraped anywhere that I could see, and I did look."

"You said Nicolas asked about Mr. Swift's hands," Mr. P. said, hiking his pants up a little higher.

I nodded. "I told him I didn't see any injuries on them. Nothing about his hands made me think he'd tried to defend himself from anyone. He wasn't cut. There were no abrasions or broken fingernails like there might have been if he had fallen and put out a hand to break the fall—that's just instinctual. I didn't see any dirt or snow on his coat or his trousers that would fit with a fall or even a heart attack. And I'm no expert, but it's hard to believe if Swift had fallen for some reason and hit his head one time on the pavement that there would be so much blood."

I laced my hands behind my head, stared up at the ceiling for a moment and blew out a breath of frustration. "Is it possible that it was all just a random act of violence?"

"I doubt it," Rose said.

I dropped my hands and looked at her and Mr. P.

"I wish it were just some senseless act, but I agree with Rosie," he said. "First of all, from what I've heard so far about the man, Vincent Swift would not have let a stranger get that close to him."

Rose nodded her agreement.

"Since you didn't see anything that looks like defensive wounds on his hands it seems that he knew the person who hit him, which is how that person got close enough to kill him in the first place."

Rose laid a hand on his arm. "We really need to

find out where that glass sphere came from," she said. "It may help us winnow down our suspect list once we have one."

I yawned. "I'm sorry," I said.

Rose bustled over to me. "It's been a long twenty-four hours. Go home. I'll see you in the morning."

I glanced over at the sink and, as so often happened, she seemed to read my mind. "Alfred and I can wash a few teacups," she said.

"Okay," I said. I headed down the hall with a dish of rhubarb, two biscuits and some custard.

When I walked into my apartment, Elvis was on the top of his cat tower. He eyed the food I was carrying and then licked his whiskers.

"This is not cat food," I said sternly.

He made a sound like a disgruntled sigh and dropped his head to his paws.

Now I felt guilty even though none of the food I was holding was suitable for a cat. I went into the kitchen, set the biscuits on the counter, put the rhubarb and the custard in the refrigerator and got Elvis a tiny bite of cheese, which cheered him up a great deal.

My phone ran while I was scratching behind the cat's right ear. He opened one green eye and meowed loudly. "Oh, is that my phone?" I said. "I thought it was yours."

The one green eye glared at me for a moment and then closed again.

It was Mac calling me. "How was the game?" I asked.

He laughed. "Way more aggressive than I expected. Cleveland called it a gentleman's hockey league but there was nothing gentlemanly about the way they played. And why, why, why didn't you tell me how competitive John is?"

"Because I didn't know. I didn't even know Cleveland had asked him to play. Gram was at Rose's and she said John might be a little competitive." Elvis nudged my hand. Just because I was holding the phone with one hand didn't mean I couldn't keep scratching behind his ear with the other.

"A little competitive?" Mac said. "He took every shot on goal as an attack on his skills—and yeah, he's pretty good—and he has a whole vocabulary of medieval swear words. Fopdoodle, sot, quisby. By the end of the game he had the whole team hollering 'fopdoodle' at the other guys!"

I laughed. "Well, at least you got some exercise and you learned some new words."

"I'm kind of afraid to find out what they all mean. There's no way 'fopdoodle' means anything good. So tell me how dessert was at Rose's."

Elvis tipped his head so I could reach his other ear. "Well, nobody yelled 'fopdoodle' at anyone else," I said.

"Count yourself lucky, then," Mac said.

"It kind of turned into an Angels' brainstorming session."

"That's a good thing, isn't it?"

"Yeah, it is," I said. "Rose gave everyone a task, so maybe we'll find some answers sooner rather than later."

"From what I heard in the locker room, people like Stella Hall a whole lot more than they did Vincent Swift."

"That's pretty much what Liz said."

"I should tell you one name I heard mentioned as having had some kind of problem with Mr. Swift."

I frowned. "Who is it?"

"Your grandmother's friend. Judge Halloran."

"Oh, c'mon," I said. "Neill Halloran is one of the kindest people I've ever met. He was a judge and yet I don't think he has an enemy. How many people who work in law enforcement can say that? I don't think he's capable of violence."

"Neither do I," Mac said. "From what I overheard, his name coming up seemed to have something to do with Mr. Swift trying to discredit Judge Halloran's abilities because he's in the very early stages of dementia."

I felt my chest tighten in anger. "Dementia or not, he's still knows more about the law than a dozen other lawyers put together." I took a breath and then a second one.

"Are you all right?" Mac asked.

"I am," I said. "Really, I am. Everything I hear about Vincent Swift makes me dislike him a little more. But it doesn't make what happened to him right. And the judge would be one of the first people to say that."

"The man's death bothers you."

I nodded, although only Elvis could see me.

"He was dying, lying half in the road, and there was nothing I could do to help him. He was alone with no one who cared about him there at the end. In the last twenty-four hours I haven't heard one person have anything good to say about the man. I think it was a sad way to die." My voice caught and I had to blink hard a couple of times.

"Vincent Swift wasn't dying alone with no one who cared about him," Mac said. "You were there. I know that you didn't know the man, but you held his hand, you told him help was coming and you urged him to hold on. You didn't have to do that, but you did. You cared about a fellow human being, and if we all have that at the end we should count ourselves lucky."

I swallowed against the sudden tightness in my throat. "What would I do without you?" I said softly.

It seemed to me that I could feel the warmth of his smile through the phone. Elvis sat up and looked at the front door. "Open your door," Mac said. "I got you a present. I hope it fits."

Still holding my phone I opened the door. Mac was standing there wearing a large gold crepe paper bow as a sash.

I threw my arms around him. "Fits perfectly," I said.

Chapter 9

I went for a short run in the morning. It was cold but there wasn't any wind and once I was moving I was glad I hadn't stayed in bed. I came back and stood under the hot spray of the shower for an extra minute to get warm again. I'd been at the shop less than half an hour when Michelle called. "I'm sorry that I didn't get back to you yesterday," she said. "Would it be all right if I stop by this morning?"

I was sitting on a stool at the workbench, sorting through a stack of old *National Geographic* magazines. "Sure," I said. "I'll be here."

"Good. It won't take long. I'll see you later."

I ended the call and put my phone back in my pocket. I eyed the stack of magazines. There was a large, nearly full cardboard box at my feet with dozens more. A man who had stopped in a couple of weeks earlier had noticed some of the *National Geographic*s that Charlotte had used between a couple of carved wooden bookends. When he got home he mentioned them to his brother. The brother, it turned out, collected the magazines. He had sent me a wish list—issues his collection was missing. He was willing to pay for FedEx shipping to Vermont, plus several dollars for each issue we had. None of them were rare or valuable and I was pleased to make a little money, with the bonus that I'd get at least some of the magazines out of the shop, and make a collector happy.

Altogether, there were two large cartons to go through. Avery and I were splitting the task because I'd discovered it was the type of job that made a person cross-eyed with boredom pretty quickly.

My phone rang again. I pulled it out of my shirt pocket and glanced at the screen. It was Jess.

"Hi," I said. "What's up?"

"I just wanted to let you know I talked to Michelle. She left about ten minutes ago. And I talked to Nick yesterday."

I rubbed one shoulder with my free hand. I already had a kink in it from leaning over the table checking the date of each magazine. "Michelle is coming here later this morning. And I talked to Nick last night."

"They can't seriously think Stella killed that man, can they?" Jess asked.

"Nick and Michelle both know Stella. I'm hoping that counts for something. But you know what Nick always says."

"'We just collect the evidence,'" we both said at the same time.

"Rose and Mr. P. and the others need to find the killer," Jess said. "The sooner the better."

"They're already looking. Rose has a plan."

"Good. I don't know what I can do to help—sew a disguise, maybe—but tell Rose if she thinks of anything to let me know."

"I will." I wasn't sure that the two of them collaborating on disguises was a good idea, though. Elvis had jumped up on the workbench. He walked over to the stack of magazines, put a paw on the top issue and pushed it to one side.

I shook my head. He gave me a defiant look and kept his foot where it was.

"Hey, Sarah, do you remember that glass ball Stella was holding? I'm pretty sure it came from the library."

"The library?" I said. Inwardly I groaned.

"Uh-huh. I think it's a crystal ball."

"You mean like a fortune-teller would use?" Elvis's paw was still on the magazine. I stood up, cradled my phone against my ear with my shoulder and picked him up, moving him down the workbench away from the magazines. He shook himself then turned his back to me and began to wash his left shoulder as though I'd given him some kind of people cooties.

"Yeah, I guess so," Jess said. "There's a display of them just across from the circulation desk. I returned some books yesterday and noticed them. What are the chances that glass ball came from somewhere else?"

"Probably not that likely."

I heard her sigh on the other end of the phone. "That kind of makes Stella look bad, doesn't it?"

"It could just be a coincidence. I'll see what Rose and Mr. P. have to say."

"You're definitely coming to the jam tomorrow night?"

Elvis was still making a show of cleaning himself and ignoring me. "I will be there," I said, "but Mac is playing poker with Mr. P. and his buddies. Nick said *he'll* try to make it."

"Oh goody!" The words had an edge of sarcasm.

"You're not going to give him a hard time about this case, are you?" I said, sitting down on the stool again.

"I may ask a question or two but that's not giving him a hard time. And why don't you tell Nick not to give *me* a hard time?"

"How do you know I haven't?"

Jess laughed. "If you did, I bet that went over well."

"You know, you and Nick are a lot alike," I said.

"In what universe?" Jess exclaimed. "He's stubborn and opinionated *and* he thinks he's always right, whereas I am determined, assertive and I pretty much always *am* right."

It was my turn to laugh.

"And I have better hair."

"I will concede the hair," I said.

"I gotta go," Jess said. "I'll see you tomorrow night, and in the meantime I'll keep my ear to the ground."

"Thanks. Everything helps."

We said good-bye and I started to put my phone in my pocket when it suddenly rang. It glanced at the screen. It was Josh. I remembered we had agreed we'd try to connect today.

"Hey, Sarah, what's up?" Josh said when I answered.

"I'm guessing you know what's up,"

"Stella told me. Please tell me no laws have been broken yet."

"Well, Rose isn't here right now so I can't promise anything."

"I think you're in that zone of deniable plausibility for the moment," he said. I could hear the smile in his voice. "I have just a few questions for you, if that's okay."

"Absolutely," I said. "Anything to help Stella." Elvis was eying the pile of *National Geographic*s once again. He moved toward them and I stuck my arm in front of him as a barrier.

"Okay, you and Jess were walking to your car Monday night."

"Yes."

"You turned the corner."

"Uh-huh."

"What did you see?"

"Vincent Swift lying in the street and Stella standing over him."

"Did you know it was Mr. Swift?" I could hear the sound of pen against paper as he made notes.

"Not until I knelt down next to him." Elvis tried to reach under my arm with one paw. I dropped my elbow to block him.

"So you knew him?" Josh asked.

Elvis tried butting my arm with his head but that didn't work, either. He yawned to show he hadn't really been interested, made his way to the far end of the workbench and jumped down to the floor.

"I knew who he was," I said. "But I don't remember ever speaking to the man."

Elvis was headed for the Angels' office. Mr. P. kept

cat treats in there for him and I pretended I didn't know.

"You recognized Stella."

"Of course." I heard the scratch of his pen again.

"Sarah, you said that Stella was standing over Vincent Swift. How close was she to him?"

I closed my eyes and tried to let the memory come to me without forcing anything. What I'd learned from Mr. P. and Rose about the unreliability of recall was fresh in my mind, and the fact that I'd told my story so many times already had made me question everything I thought I knew about that night. "Three, maybe four feet. It looked like she was closer because she was standing."

"What did you do?"

I explained that I'd realized Stella was in shock and how Jess had called for help and taken care of Stella while I tried to help Mr. Swift.

Josh asked a couple more questions then he said, "That should do it for now. Is there anything you need?"

"There is one thing," I said. "I'm looking for information on the lawsuit that Mr. Swift filed against the state after the accident in which Madison Telfer was killed. Do you remember any of the details?"

He sighed. "I remember it was messy situation," he said. "I wasn't involved personally, but I did use that case in a class I taught. I have a meeting in few minutes, but if you can stop by after lunch—say, around one o'clock—I can tell you what I know."

"I'll be there," I said. "Thanks. I don't know what we'd do without you."

Josh laughed. "Anytime, Sarah. Working with the Angels keeps life from getting boring."

"We live to serve," I said. "I'll see you after lunch."

I put the pile of magazines I hadn't gotten to back in the box on the floor and turned another carton upside done over the ones I'd pulled for the customer just in case Elvis came back to nose around.

There were no customers in the shop. Charlotte was packing a couple of orders from the website. "I'll be in my office," I said. "Yell if you need me."

I stopped in the workroom and got a cup of coffee, then I sat down at my desk and opened my laptop. I didn't really know that much about the car accident that had led to Vincent Swift's lawsuit against the state. I wanted to learn a few more details before I saw Josh. I didn't want to waste his time asking about things I could discover online.

The first thing I did was go to the newspaper's archives. There were several articles about the accident. I clicked on the first one and read the details. The SUV had gone off the road and turned upside down. Two people had been injured—Jacob Pena and Vincent Swift—and one had died—Madison Telfer. At the time the authorities didn't know what had caused the crash but it had been snowing, it was dark and other drivers had said that visibility was poor.

My heart sank at the sight of the photograph that went along with the article. It showed the SUV resting on its roof in the ditch. There was damage to the back passenger side and the window had been smashed, either by the accident or the first responders trying to get Madison out of the SUV. Lights from the rescue vehicles reflecting off the road made the pavement look slick.

A second photograph showed one lone black Converse high-top next to the roof of the upside down vehicle. Jacob's shoe or maybe Madison's. A fine layer of snow covered the ground and the SUV. My stomach clenched and I pressed a hand to my chest and took a couple of slow breaths.

I clicked on a link that would take me to a story about the lawsuit. The details were simple: Vincent Swift and Jacob Pena's parents, on behalf of their son, had sued the state for damages due to the negligence of the road crew the night of the accident claiming, just as Mr. P. had said, that they hadn't treated the road the way they should have and they'd spent too long on their break. Scanning the letters to the editor as the lawsuit proceeded confirmed that for the most part sentiment was pretty much split down the middle, with slightly more people blaming the road crew. Some of the things that were said about the men were ugly, and there were equally disgusting things said about Jacob. As Liz had told us, the jury sided with the plaintiffs and awarded each of them a million and a half dollars. The state then offered a settlement. They would give up the right to appeal if Vincent Swift and Jacob Pena would take a lesser amount of money. The details were kept private but there were rumors of a six-figure payout for both of them.

I shut down my laptop. Somehow when the lawsuit was happening I had missed how much anger it had stirred up. I couldn't imagine how agonizing it must have been for Madison's mother and father.

I went back downstairs. Mr. P. was at his desk in the Angels' office. Elvis was *on* the desk with a couple of crumbs stuck to his whiskers, but there was no sign of Rose.

"How's your morning going?" Mr. P. asked.

"Michelle should be here soon. I'm going to talk to Josh right after lunch. And I learned something that might be important from Jess. Is Rose around?"

He shook his head. "She's gone to the library to do a little sleuthing. What did Jess tell you?"

One again I perched on the corner of his desk. "Jess told me the same thing Rose is probably finding out right now. It looks like that glass ball Stella was holding on to came from a display at the library."

Mr. P. pursed his lips for a moment. "That should have occurred to me. I knew their theme this month is Fortune and Fate. They were also planning a display about palmistry and a workshop about reading tarot cards and of course showcasing books on the subjects." He noticed my confusion about how he knew all of this. "I receive the library's monthly email blast. You should consider signing up. There's so much happening in the building in any given week. I'll send you the signup link."

"Umm, thank you," I said.

"And I'll text Rosie in a minute and let her know what you found out just in case."

I pulled a folded piece of paper out of my pocket and handed it to him. "This is the route Jess and I walked on the way to the car."

Mr. P. smiled. "Thank you. I already talked to Sam and he had video from the pub's security camera that he sent along to me. I found you and Jess heading along the boardwalk."

"Does the video show anyone else?"

"Alas, it doesn't. But now that I know exactly where you were walking, I'm sure I'll be able to find more video."

There was a sheet of paper on his desk. I recognized Charlotte's precise printing. "Is that the Swift family tree? I asked.

"It is," Mr. P. said.

"May I?" I asked.

He nodded. "Of course." He picked up the piece of paper and handed it to me.

I studied the names and the connections between them. "If I'm reading it correctly, Daniel Swift and Vincent Swift were third cousins."

"They were." Mr. P. said.

I had met Daniel Swift three times. I'd known who he was, of course. I'd seen him around North Harbor and heard his name mentioned. He was a tall, imposing man with a lined face from years of being out on the water—he loved to sail. Our first, brief meeting happened because both he and Gram had been involved with the renovations to the Opera House. The second time we met was when Liz and I had gone to see Daniel at Swift Holdings.

Daniel Swift was at his desk, but he stood up and came around to take Liz's hand in his own. He had a very slight limp, I noticed, but he was still a formidable man. He looked every inch the successful businessman.

My third encounter with the man had been interrupted by Rose. Things had not gone well. For him.

Daniel had been condescending and self-absorbed. Which seemed to be words that described Vincent Swift as well.

I shook my head, trying to get rid of the memory. "Daniel Swift wasn't a very nice person," I said to Mr. P.

He shook his head. "I'm sorry to say it appears that quality runs in the family."

Chapter 10

"I'll let you know what I find out from Josh," I promised Mr. P. I leaned over and gave Elvis a scratch on the top of his furry head. He licked the side of my hand as if to say I was forgiven for the whole magazines incident.

"And I'll keep working on tracking down William Swift," Mr. P. said.

"I have faith in your skills."

He raised an eyebrow. "Some people would say it's better to be lucky than good."

I smiled. "I'll take good any day, but if you happen to have a little luck in your back pocket that works for me, too."

I decided I'd run out to talk to Mac in the workshop before I went back to the shop. I wanted to ask him about a fireplace mantel I'd seen listed for sale on Facebook. It had been painted flat black and I was pretty sure that the top had been covered in strips of zebra-patterned duct tape, but the piece had some nice details from what I could see in the two photos and the price was a steal. I didn't have my coat but the sun was shining and it wasn't windy. And if I were cold when I got there Mac would just have to warm me up.

As I opened the door, Michelle drove into the parking lot. I raised a hand in hello as she got out of the car and waited in the doorway while she walked over to join me. She wore a hooded navy blue parka with a navy beanie and a forest green scarf at her neck. She held up a small paper bag. "Blueberry muffins from Glenn," she said.

Glenn McNamara ran McNamara's Sandwich Shop. He made great sandwiches and treats, the blueberry muffins being my favorite.

"Thank you," I said. "C'mon up to my office and I'll get us coffee."

We headed for the shop, trailed by Elvis, who had appeared as soon as Michelle stepped inside the door. I was betting he had somehow smelled the muffins.

Charlotte was at the cash desk wrapping a length of snowy white linen in a piece of acid-free tissue. The cloth had turned up in a tea chest that Teresa Reynard, another of the pickers I regularly bought from, had found at a flea market. Teresa had assumed the long piece of fabric was a tablecloth, but Charlotte had immediately recognized its true use. It was a communion cloth. The name *St. Alban's* had been embroidered in delicate white-on-white stitches at both ends of the fabric. It turned out the cloth had been stolen years earlier from a little church across the border in nearby New Brunswick. Charlotte, with a lot of help from Avery and Mr. P., had contacted the minister, and now the cloth was going back to the congregation. Michelle had cleared things with the Royal Canadian Mounted Police, who had found the thief but hadn't recovered everything he'd stolen.

Michelle stopped at the desk. "Is that the communion cloth?" she asked.

Charlotte nodded. "It's on its way home, finally."

"I like a happy ending," Michelle said with a smile. "We don't always get them."

We headed up to my office and I got coffee for both of us and two sardine crackers for Elvis. The cat had decided he wanted to sit next to Michelle on the small purple love seat Mac and I had moved upstairs a couple of weeks ago.

"Elvis, get down," I said as I set Michelle's mug on the end of my desk.

"He's fine, Sarah," she said. She reached over to stroke his fur and he began to purr, the two sardine crackers forgotten for the moment.

I sat down in my chair and took a sip of my coffee. Then once again I recounted what had happened Monday night.

Michelle gave Elvis a scratch behind one ear but kept her attention on me. He turned *his* attention to the sardine crackers.

"So Mr. Swift didn't move or speak."

"He didn't. At first I thought he was dead but then I found his pulse and realized he was breathing."

"What did you do next?"

"There wasn't anything to do. Jess had called 911. I, uh, I just held his hand and told him to hang on." Knowing Vincent Swift had been taking his last breaths and there hadn't been anything I could do was going to bother me for a while.

"How did Stella seem to you?" Michelle asked.

"It seemed like she was in shock," I said. "She was very pale and a little shaky."

"Did you see anyone else?"

I shook my head slowly. "I didn't. But I was focused on Stella and Mr. Swift. I could have missed something or someone."

"Okay," she said. She reached for her coffee and took a sip. "Oh, this is so much better than the station coffee."

"That's Mr. P.'s doing," I said. "You've heard of a wine connoisseur? He's a coffee connoisseur."

"Alfred Peterson has a lot of skills."

I smiled. "Just when I think I know the man, I learn something new. He played football, you know. And he was a Boy Scout."

Elvis was sniffing around the love seat, whiskers twitching, looking for more crackers.

"The Boy Scout part doesn't surprise me, but the playing football does a little bit."

I laughed. "It did me, too."

"I'm assuming some of Alfred's skills are being used to investigate Vincent Swift's murder." The sentence wasn't worded in the form of a question.

"They are."

"If he or anyone else comes up with anything . . ." She didn't finish the sentence. She didn't need to.

"If Rose doesn't call you, I'll call you myself."

Elvis put his two front paws on Michelle's knee

and looked expectantly at her. She broke off a tiny bite of her muffin and fed it to him. I pretended not to notice. "I'm sorry if I'm putting you in a bad spot," she said.

"Any spot I'm in is of my own making." I held out both hands. "Their office is here. I drive them wherever they need to go. I let myself get sucked into doing things."

"Maybe you should get your private investigator's license."

I laughed. "Don't even joke about that. Nick's head would literally explode. I know he's trying to be openminded but he'd be happier if his mother and Rose and the rest of them would go back to organizing bake sales for the hot lunch program."

Michelle smiled. "He's a good guy, but Nick can be a little rigid."

"I think this case worries him a little more because Stella is a friend. You know how Rose is when a case gets personal."

"I do," she said, "and that worries me a little, too."

"I'll keep an eye on Rose, I promise," I said. "And Mr. P. is very sensible."

"Just be careful, okay?"

I nodded. "I will."

She picked up her mug and drank the last of her coffee.

"I'm guessing you know that Swift made some enemies with that lawsuit against the state a couple of years ago," I said. My own mug was empty.

"One thing I've learned in this job is that hard feelings last a long time." Michelle patted her pocket as though she was checking to make sure her phone was there. "Have you found Swift's son yet?"

I ran a hand over the back of my head. "No, but Mr. P. is on it."

"It's heartbreaking when a child and a parent are so at odds that the child changes their name and moves away. I can't wrap my mind around it. Choosing to be separated from your family because your life seems better that way." She sighed softly.

I realized she was thinking about her own father, who had been dead since we were teenagers. It took another moment before I realized she had just given me a small piece of information that might help the Angels' investigation.

Michelle glanced at her watch. It had belonged to her father and I knew wearing it made her feel close to him. "I need to get back to the station," she said. She gave Elvis one last scratch on the top of his furry head and got to her feet, brushing a bit of cat hair off her black-and-gray-checked trousers.

I came around the side of the desk. "I promise I'll keep you in the loop."

She nodded, and then hesitated. "I kind of need a favor," she said.

I smiled. "Sure. What is it?"

"I want to buy a house. I'm tired of living in an apartment. I want a yard. I want something that's mine. When this case is over and it's a bit closer to spring, will you help me look? You have a lot more experience than I do."

"I'd love to help," I said. "What are you thinking about?"

She made a face. "I'm not really sure. Mostly something that's not too big and with enough space for a little garden."

"Okay, that gives us a place to start. And think about picking Liam's brain next time he's in town. He'll have opinions and won't be afraid to share them."

"Thank you," she said. She gave me a quick hug and we headed downstairs. I walked Michelle out and then poked my head in the sunporch to update Mr. P. on what I'd learned about Vincent Swift's son.

"Knowing that William changed his name is very helpful," he said. "And I spoke to Rose, and Jess is correct. It appears the murder weapon did come from the library. They're missing a fortune-teller's ball from their display and it matches the one you described."

I felt a sinking sensation in my stomach and it must have shown on my face.

"Don't worry, my dear," Mr. P. said. "All that means is that we now know the killer was at the library. That will give us a smaller pool of suspects, that's all."

Liz dropped off Rose and Avery at lunchtime. "Nonna told me to give you this," Avery said, handing Mr. P. a folded sheet of paper. It was a list of people who'd had issues with Vincent Swift in the last five years. The time frame was an arbitrary number Rose had decided on. Rose had also made a list of what had been going on at the library Monday night.

"I'll cross-reference and see if there's anyone on

Elizabeth's list who is connected to anything that was happening at the library," Mr. P. said. "It's a place to start."

"I'm going to see Josh right after lunch," I told Rose. "Maybe I'll learn something that will help."

I arrived at the building where Josh had his law office at five to one. He was waiting for me in the reception area. "It's good to see you, Sarah," he said. He gestured toward his open office door. "C'mon in."

The building where Josh's office was located was over a hundred years old but had been beautifully restored. His office had high ceilings, a huge walnut desk, and a bank of windows that let the sun flood the space. Floor-to-ceiling bookshelves filled the wall to the left, with a rolling library ladder to reach the highest shelves. On the right was a wall of exposed brick. In front of the desk there was a large Oriental rug in shades of navy, red and gold covering part of the oak floor. Josh had gotten new chairs since the last time I'd been in his office. There were two dove gray leather tub chairs in front of his desk and four more around a glass and metal round table next to the brick wall.

Josh gestured to the table. "Have a seat," he said. There was a pad of yellow paper and a pen on the table in front of one of the chairs so I picked the one opposite it.

Josh Evans was tall and lean, and Rose was always trying to fatten him up. He'd worn his sandy hair in the same short, spiky style for more than twenty years. He still wore black-framed glasses like the ones he'd had when he was a kid, but at least now they weren't held together at one corner with silver duct tape. He wasn't wearing his suit jacket and his tie was loose. He'd rolled back the sleeves of his crisp, white shirt and I noticed he was wearing his *Darkwing Duck* watch. Josh had been obsessed with the purple-suited carton superhero when we were kids. Seeing the watch brought back happy memories of all the summers I'd spent in North Harbor with Gram.

"You want more information about the lawsuit Vincent Swift filed against the state," he said, taking his seat at the table.

I nodded. "Yes."

"What do you know?"

"I know that Swift sued the state because the road crew hadn't treated the section of road where the accident occurred. They were behind schedule. His lawyers claimed that was why the accident had happened. They said there was black ice on the road."

"That's right. The road crew had a schedule to follow with respect to treating the highway—subject to weather, of course. It wasn't written in stone, but they were expected to stay on that schedule."

"So what went wrong?"

He picked up the pen in front of him and turned it over in his fingers. "They were only fifteen minutes late getting back after their break, but there *was* ice on the road and a bit of snow over it. Swift's lawyers made the case that if the road crew had stuck to their timetable they would have treated the road and the ice would have melted."

I shook my head. "Fifteen minutes? The whole lawsuit was based on such a short amount of time? I don't understand. Was the crew really negligent?"

Josh made a face. "The jury thought so. The guy driving the salt truck had just told the others that he was going to be a dad. His girlfriend was pregnant. They were congratulating him and scaring him a bit with stories about babies who never sleep. The waitress and the other people in the diner remembered one of the plow drivers getting up and giving a little speech. Since they used a debit card the lawyers could show exactly what time they left the place."

"So did they have any sort of explanation?"

"The supervisor insisted they were late starting their break in the first place because of the traffic in front of them and the others agreed, but no one could prove that and Swift's lawyers argued they all had reason to protect each other."

I blew out a breath. "I'd forgotten that part of the story," I said.

Josh nodded. "So had I. After I talked to you this morning I looked back through my class notes to refresh my memory. One thing that didn't help, about six months before the accident a supervisor and three workers had lost their jobs for padding their overtime. There were a lot of hard feelings about that. It made it easier for everyone to believe the guys were lying to protect themselves this time. I think that, and the fact that Madison Telfer died, influenced the jury."

I frowned. "What do you mean?"

"It doesn't matter how hard people try to be fair. We have biases we're not even aware that are coming in to play. And don't forget, in a civil case it's not proof beyond a reasonable doubt that decides the outcome. It's a preponderance of evidence. In other words, the jury believes there is a greater than fifty percent chance that the claim is true."

"But that's so . . . subjective."

He nodded again. "Yes. In some ways it is. The jury awarded Swift and Jacob Pena a million and a half dollars each. But the state ended up paying out less."

"Because they offered an immediate payout?" I asked.

"Yes. The state gave up their right to appeal the verdict and in return they paid out less than the jury had awarded. It meant the money wasn't tied up for years."

"A bird in the hand."

"Exactly," Josh said. "And Brent LeBlanc and Earle Weyman lost their jobs."

I stared at him. "Wait a minute. I know both of them. Earle does a little picking with Cleveland sometimes. And Brent used to work maintenance at the Bluebird Motel."

I pictured Earle Weyman. He was a large block of a man with ruddy skin, bushy eyebrows and a face that seemed more than a little scary until he smiled. He looked like the kind of person who could rip a tree stump out of the ground with his bare hands—which he could; I'd seen it. I'd also seen him slide across cracking lake ice to rescue a dog that had fallen through.

Brent LeBlanc was quiet with a shy smile. He was a lot stronger than his skinny frame suggested.

"Knowing them could work to your advantage," Josh said. "They're a lot more likely to talk to you."

"What about Madison Telfer's parents?" I asked. "Nick said they weren't part of the lawsuit."

Josh tapped the end of the pen he'd been holding on the pad of paper in front of him. "They weren't. Her father, Damian, was very vocal in his belief that Jacob Pena and Vincent Swift were the reason his daughter had died."

"Do you know why?"

"Jacob wasn't the first teenage boy—or girl—who drove too fast." He gave me a wry smile. "I know I did."

I nodded. "So did I."

"Madison's parents weren't too crazy about her being in a car with Jacob because he'd already been caught speeding once out on that stretch of road that goes to Swift Hills. Damian also blamed Vincent Swift because Swift knew that about the speeding ticket—he'd somehow gotten it down to a warning—but he still let Jacob drive his SUV that night."

"What about Damian Telfer's wife?" I asked.

Josh looked past me for a moment then his gaze returned to my face. "From what I've been able to find out, she was more grief-stricken than angry. I heard that she went to visit Jacob in the hospital. That she forgave him. She didn't seem to feel the same amount of animosity toward Swift, either."

It struck me that Damian Telfer, at least, should go on the suspect list. "The whole thing was ugly," I said.

"It was," Josh agreed. "And a lot of the wounds are still raw. This time especially, the Angels need to be careful. If they come up with anything, call me right away. I don't want any problems if Stella ends up being charged."

"Do you think she will?" I asked. That worry seemed to be lodged in my chest like a stitch in my side from running too fast.

Josh set his pen on the table. "I'm going to do my best to keep that from happening." He grinned then. "Remember, 'I am the terror that flaps in the night!'"

I couldn't help smiling at Darkwing Duck's catchphrase. But it really didn't make the worry go away.

Chapter 11

I drove back to Second Chance thinking about what I'd learned from Josh. The more I found out about Vincent Swift, the less I liked the man. I kept hoping I'd discover that he secretly fostered abandoned kittens or volunteered with the hot lunch program but that hadn't happened.

I stopped at the old garage to talk to Mac. He was re-caning the bottom of a nursery rocking chair. "That's going to be really nice when it's finished," I said. The low, armless rocker had been painted a pale buttery yellow and I could picture it in the shop with a couple of teddy bears and possibly a friendly black cat on the seat.

Mac straightened up, wiping his hands on his paint-smeared jeans. "Thanks," he said. "Who would have thought I'd go to a poker game, win twenty-five dollars and learn how to do this?"

I grinned. "You're no slouch when it comes to poker, but given the fact that you were playing with

Mr. P. and his friends the more likely outcome would be that you lost money."

Mac grinned back at me. "Those guys are a bunch of card sharks, no question." He rubbed at a smear of black paint on his wrist. "According to Rose, there are a couple of casinos in Las Vegas that Sheldon has been banned from."

Sheldon Hammerback was a former optometrist with wild hair like Albert Einstein and sharp brown eyes that watched everything, everywhere. He enjoyed poker and liked to go to Las Vegas or Atlantic City a couple times a year to play. He always seemed to come back happy. Once he'd come back with a waitress who had lasted several months, until the first nor'easter blew through.

"I believe that," I said. I was surprised, though, that he knew how to cane a chair.

"The combined knowledge of those men would scare you," Mac said. "If they wanted to build a giant robot and take over the world they could do it."

I cocked an eyebrow at him. "I'm not worried. I'm on Team Rose. She'd stage a bloodless coup and make cookies for everyone afterward."

Mac put an arm around my shoulder and kissed the top of my head. "I'm so glad I answered your ad. I thought I was just going to get a job that would allow me to stay in North Harbor and sail, and instead I got the job, I got you and I got this crazy, unpredictable, wonderful group of people who turned into family."

"That last one is a legally binding relationship that

requires you to show up anytime anyone is moving and to always have bail money and teabags," I said.

"Anytime and always," Mac said. I laid my head on his shoulder for a moment. "How did your meeting go with Josh?" he asked.

"On the plus side, I don't think Stella is in any danger of being arrested anytime soon." I straightened up and tucked my hair behind one ear.

"Well, that's good. What's the downside?"

"You know the big guy who sometimes helps Cleveland now that his cousin seems to have disappeared? Big hands. Big bushy eyebrows." I put my hand on my left upper arm. 'Has a tattoo of a snake right here."

"You mean Earle Weyman?"

I nodded. "He's the supervisor who lost his job when Swift sued the state."

Mac exhaled loudly and shook his head. "I can't say I know the man but he seems like a good guy."

"Cleveland wouldn't work with anyone who isn't."

"He should be by here in the next day or so." I knew he meant Cleveland. "Are you going to talk to him about Earle?"

"I was, but do you think it might be better to let Mr. P. do it?" Cleveland and his brother, Memphis, had helped with security while the Angels were investigating the goings-on at a cat show. Elvis had gone undercover as a contestant and Cleveland and Mr. P. has gotten to know each other a lot better.

Mac bent down and brushed a bit of cat hair from the half-finished seat of the rocking chair. "I think you've known Cleveland for quite a while and you know Earle. Alfred doesn't. I think you should talk to Cleveland."

I nodded. His logic made sense.

"Did you find anything else about the salt truck driver?" he said.

I unzipped my coat. I was getting warm. "You know how they say we're all just six connections away from anyone else?"

"I've heard the theory."

"I know the salt truck driver. I'm fairly certain Rose does as well. Do you remember when the Bluebird Motel was being renovated?"

"Yeah. They sold a bunch of stuff they'd had in storage for years. We got some furniture."

"Do you remember me coming back and telling you about the kid who had helped me load it all?"

"Brent something or other. We saw him at a flea market sometime in the fall, didn't we? Blond hair. Skinny."

I stuffed my hands in my pockets. The rest of me was too warm but they were cold. "Brent LeBlanc. He was driving the salt truck."

Mac frowned. "He didn't look like he was that much older than Avery," he said.

"He's not, really. He'd be twenty-four, maybe twenty-five."

"And you think he's one of Rose's former students?"

I nodded. "When I mentioned him after I came back from the motel, she thought she'd taught him for one year. I think the family moved or Brent might have just stopped showing up for school. I need to see if Mr. P. can find him, then maybe Rose and I could go talk to him." I linked my fingers together and slid my hands back over my head and onto my neck. "I hate this part," I said. "I hate it when someone I know is a suspect."

"Not a suspect," Mac said. "Just someone you need to talk to." He was always the voice of reason. "For all you know, Brent was home on his couch with a beer and a meatball sub watching the hockey game."

"I hope you're right." I stretched my head backward for a moment, trying to work out the kink in my neck, and then unlaced my fingers and let my arms fall to my sides. "Mac, do you see a big burly man like Earle hitting Vincent Swift with a fortune-teller's crystal ball? Or Brent doing it, for that matter?"

"I don't. Why would either one of them even have been holding a fortune-teller's ball in the first place?"

That's a question I'd been asking myself. What had the killer been doing with that crystal ball?

"I don't mean to sound like a jerk," Mac continued, "but I'd most likely have punched the guy in the nose. And I wouldn't have waited so long to do it. Most of the guys I know—with maybe the exception of Mr. P.—are more likely to lead with a fist—which isn't always a good idea." He shrugged. "It's just a guy thing."

"I'll keep that in mind," I said. I pulled the piece of paper with the information about the mantel I was interested in out of my pocket. "What do you think about this?"

He studied the picture. "Do you think that's wallpaper on the top?"

"More likely duct tape. But I think I can get it off."

"If it's wood and not some cheap papier-mâché, it looks like it would be worth the effort to refinish." He looked up at me. "I could go check it out, and if it seems like a good deal I'll buy it."

I stood on tiptoes and kissed him. "Thank you," I said.

He smiled. "I've got this covered. Go do detective stuff."

Mr. P. wasn't in the Angels' office. Avery was sitting at the workbench sorting more of the magazines. "If you're looking for Mr. P., he went somewhere," she said without looking up.

"Do you know where?" I said.

She shrugged. "Nope." There were two *National Geographic* magazines off to her right. She picked them up and looked over her shoulder at me. "Can I have these? Please? They're not on the list. You can check."

"I believe you," I said. "Go ahead. Take them."

She smiled. "Thanks. And can I have that old chandelier that's out in the garage?"

"Do you mean the one that's painted blue?"

She nodded. "Yeah. That one."

"It doesn't work. It needs to be rewired."

"I don't care. It doesn't have to work."

The light fixture had been out in the workshop for ages. I figured it would cost more to get it looking good and working properly than I'd ever make in a sale but I hated to just toss it out. "Are you going to use it in your window display?" I asked.

Avery shook her head. "No. I need it for something else."

"All right. You can have it. Just remember the wiring doesn't work."

"I know," she said with just an edge of annoyance in her voice. "I'm not going to try to make it work and burn Nonna's house down. I swear."

"All right," I said. "Where's Rose?"

She jerked her head in the direction of the shop. "With a customer."

Rose—and Elvis, it seemed—were helping a customer measure a curved ceramic side table. The first time I'd seen it I'd thought it resembled a drawing of the bones of the middle ear that had been in my eleventh-grade biology textbook.

I was about to go up to my office when a slightly frazzled-looking woman came in. She wore a quilted red coat, yoga pants, and nothing on her hands. Her hair was in a lopsided, messy bun.

I smiled at her. "Is there something I could help you with?"

"I hope so," she said. "My daughter has changed all her wedding plans and wants to get married at home in *two weeks* with a reception at home in *two weeks*." She brushed a stray strand of hair away from her face. "I need wineglasses for the toast and plates for the buffet and forks and spoons and a really nice tablecloth and none of the rental places can help because it's happening in *two weeks* and nobody we know has any of those things because who entertains anymore?" She blurted the whole thing out in one run-on sentence without taking a breath.

"How many people there will be?" I asked, crossing my fingers that the number wouldn't be too large.

"Twenty-five." She looked at me, lips pressed together, one thumb picking at the skin on the thumb of her other hand.

Twenty-five. That we could do. "I think we can help you." I said.

The woman's shoulders sagged with relief. "Thank you," she said. "I'm usually not this frazzled but I was running out of options. And I'm Cynthia, by the way."

I smiled again. "I'm Sarah. Tell me about the reception."

"It's buffet style, mostly finger food."

"That makes it easier," I said. "Give me a minute." I got Avery and sent her for several bins of dishes that were in the workroom. We managed to find enough of everything. I didn't have twenty-five identical wineglasses but I did have a dozen of one design and fourteen of another very similar pattern. By this time Rose had sold the ceramic table and the woman who had bought it and I carried it out to her car, set it on the front seat and belted it in place. I crossed my fingers she'd get it home in one piece.

When I walked back inside, Avery was explaining to Cynthia how to dress the table. The panicked look was back on the woman's face. "I'm no good at anything creative like that," Cynthia said. "I'll pay you a hundred dollars if you'll come to my house and do it the day of the wedding."

Avery shook her head. "One hundred dollars is way too much for something that will only take maybe an hour, hour and a half at the most."

"Okay. Ninety-five," Cynthia said.

They went back and forth and ended up settling at seventy-five dollars.

Avery found a tablecloth and a runner and two vases that the woman also bought. They exchanged cell phone numbers and Avery made a note of the date of the wedding in her phone. We packed everything in boxes and carried them out to Cynthia's car.

"Thank you doesn't seem like enough," she said and then she hugged me.

"Enjoy the wedding, and if you think of anything else you need, please come back."

"I will," she said.

I waved as she drove away, thinking how good it felt to have a problem I could solve so easily.

Chapter 12

I walked back inside. Rose was just putting the lid on the remaining bin of dishes, which Avery picked up.

"Thank you for all your help," I said to her.

"No problem," she said with a shrug but I noticed just a hint of a smile on her face as she headed out to the workroom.

"Thank you for your help, too," I said to Rose.

She smiled. "Anytime, sweetie. I think organizing a wedding would be fun."

I arched an eyebrow. "Mr. P. would make a very handsome groom."

"Never you mind about that," she said sternly, swatting my arm, but I could see she was fighting a smile.

"Where is Mr. P.?" I asked.

"He went to the courthouse. He said he'd explain later."

"Something to do with Stella's case?"

She smoothed a wrinkle from the front of her

apron. "I'm assuming so. He said he'd be back before the end of the day."

"So did you learn anything at the library this morning?"

"Everyone likes Stella," she said. "But we already knew that."

I nodded.

"I started wondering about something, though. Where was the driver?"

I looked uncertainly at her. "What driver?"

"Vincent Swift's. You said that Stella told the first police officer that his driver always picked him up."

"That's right. She did say that. She said he didn't drive anymore. Not since the accident. It didn't really register at the time."

"It's all right," Rose said. "I missed it, too. So did Alfred. But where was the car? And where was the driver?"

I made an aimless gesture with one hand. "I don't know. Maybe it never showed up. Maybe Swift got mad at the driver and got out. Maybe the driver had an accident."

"Well, I think we should find out."

"Michelle might know," I said.

"Do you really think she'd tell us?"

I shook my head. "No, she wouldn't." She'd already given us a clue by letting it slip that William Swift had changed his name. I didn't see her sharing anything else. "What about Nick?"

Rose bent down and picked up a scrap of tissue paper from the floor. "I don't think it's exactly his bailiwick."

"When Mr. P. comes back maybe he could find something."

"I'm certain he could . . ." The end of the sentence trailed away, and I saw a gleam in her eye as something pinged in the back of my mind.

"Liz." We both spoke at the same time.

"If she doesn't know anything she'll know someone who does," I said.

"Or she'll put Jane Evans on the case."

I pulled my phone out of my pocket. "Do you want me to call her?"

Rose nodded. "Please."

Jane answered the phone at Liz's office. "Liz is in a meeting at the moment," she said. "She'll probably be a half an hour or so. She's not a big fan of long meetings. Would you like her to call you back?"

I mouthed the word "meeting" at Rose, who made a face.

"Could I leave her a message?" I asked.

"You could," Jane said. "What is it?"

"I'm trying to find Vincent Swift's driver. I was wondering if Liz knows his name or which company he works for."

"I don't know the man's name," Jane said. "But I can tell you he works for Midcoast Transportation. That was the car service Mr. Swift used. I could certainly find out the driver's name for you." She lowered her voice a little. "Liz's name opens quite a few doors. It's my superpower."

"That's a lot of power, Jane," I said. "Use it wisely."

She laughed. "Let me see what I can find out for you."

I thanked her and ended the call.

"Jane is on the case," I said to Rose. "She already knew the name of the car service and I have no doubt she'll find out the driver's name. And I'm not going to worry about how she does that."

Rose patted my arm. "Very wise. If you're going to eat the sausage, you shouldn't watch how it's made."

Jane called me back about twenty minutes later. "The driver's name is Guy Tremblay. 'Guy' is pronounced the French way with a long *E* sound, not a long *I* sound. He was the only driver Mr. Swift used in the last year. And he will be there to talk to you in about fifteen minutes."

"Thank you, Jane," I said. "Does he know why we want to talk to him?"

"He knows that you're investigating Mr. Swift's death. He's happy to help if he can."

I wondered how Jane had managed to make all of this happen so quickly. Then I remembered what Rose had said and decided I didn't need to know what had gone into this metaphorical sausage.

Guy Tremblay showed up exactly fourteen minutes later. "I'm looking for Ms. Grayson and Mrs. Jackson," he said. He was a stocky man, early fifties, I guessed, with dark-framed glasses and iron gray hair in a brush cut. He wore an unzipped navy blue winter jacket over black pants, a pale blue shirt and a darker blue vest with a blue tie. I wondered if the clothes were the company uniform.

Rose smiled and offered her hand. "Mr. Tremblay, thank you for coming," she said. "I'm Rose Jackson and this is Sarah Grayson."

"It's a pleasure to meet you both," he said. I heard what sounded like a trace of a French accent.

"Please, come back to my office," Rose said. We left Avery in charge and Rose led the way to the sun-porch. She'd gone upstairs and made a pot of tea while we were waiting because it was one of the ways she put people at ease, I'd come to realize. And because she'd use any excuse to have a cup herself.

We sat at one end of the long table. Rose offered Mr. Tremblay a cup of tea, which he accepted.

"You have some questions about Mr. Swift," he said after Rose had poured for all three of us. If he thought it was odd that the private investigator he'd been sent to talk to was a sweet, gray-haired lady offering him tea, he didn't let on.

"How long had you been his driver?" Rose asked.

"Just over a year."

"So you drove him wherever he wanted to go?"

Tremblay nodded. "I took him to his office in the morning. I drove him home at the end of the day. I got him to and from whatever appointments he had. He kept a fairly regular schedule."

"You didn't pick him up from the library on Monday night," I said. "Why?"

He took a sip of his tea. "I had a problem with the car. The wheel came off."

I frowned. "You had a flat tire?"

He shook his head. "No, the actual wheel came off. It's a good thing I was at the on-ramp and not on the highway. I did have a flat the week before. This was a new tire."

"They should have torqued the nuts after you'd driven on it for a few days," Rose said.

"It's possible that was the problem."

I traced the rim of my cup with one finger. "Did you call Mr. Swift?" I asked.

He nodded. "I left him a message. I knew he wouldn't answer his phone or even look at it in a meeting. And I called the office to send someone else to pick him up."

"But no one showed up."

His face tightened. "The driver was new. Unfortunately, he got lost."

"What was Mr. Swift like to work for?" Rose asked.

Mr. Tremblay shrugged. "I didn't have any problems with him. Being on time was important to him, but it is to me, too, so that part worked out fine. He didn't talk much, well, most of the time, but that didn't bother me."

Rose tipped her head to one side. "Most of the time?"

"All the time, really," he said, "except last week, I think it was Thursday. He asked me if I'd married my first love."

Rose and I exchanged a look.

"What did you say?" she said.

"I said no. I married my last love. I married the woman I'm gonna grow old with. He told me I was lucky. I said he was right. But it also took hard work to have a strong marriage and I was proud that we'd both done the work."

"How long have you been married?" I asked.

"Twenty-four years on Valentine's Day." He smiled. "It helps to get married on a date that's hard to forget."

"Did Mr. Swift say anything else?" Rose asked.

Tremblay's expression turned thoughtful. "He asked me if I ever thought about roads not taken. I asked him if he meant that literally or if he was talking about roads in life. He said the second one. I told him there was no point in wasting time on what's already done. He said, 'Wouldn't you want to know for certain?' I said I wasn't sure. Maybe. That was the end of it."

This was not the conversation I'd expected to have. Everything I knew up to this point about Vincent Swift didn't make him seem like a man given to introspection about roads not taken. Rose looked at me and I shook my head. I didn't have any more questions.

She thanked Mr. Tremblay for coming to talk to us and showed him out. When she came back to the office I was still sitting at the table, turning my cup in slow circles on its saucer, trying to make sense of this new information.

"Well, that was certainly interesting," she said, taking her seat again. She felt the side of the teapot in its quilted cozy and then poured herself another cup. She looked at me and I shook my head.

"It was weird," I said. "I don't mean Mr. Tremblay. He was a very nice man. I mean learning that Vincent Swift seemed to be second-guessing his life choices just days before he died. Do you think it matters?"

Rose added a little sugar to her tea. "You mean do I think it has anything to do with his death?"

I stopped playing with the teacup and put both hands flat on the table. "Yes. It sounds like the plot of a bad movie-of-the-week."

"I don't know," she said. She took a sip of her tea. "But you want to find out, don't you?"

I leaned back in my chair, rested my head against the wall behind me and closed my eyes. "Whether somehow the man's past caught up with him or he just happened to be thinking about his regrets days before he died, either option seems like a pretty big coincidence."

She didn't say anything so I opened my eyes and looked across the table at her. "This is where you're supposed to tell me that I should do some digging and find out whether Vincent Swift's past somehow ended his future."

She nodded. "That does sound like something I'd say. So is that what you're going to do?"

It was probably a waste of time. There were probably better ways of helping Stella.

"Yes," I said. "I am."

Rose smiled. "Well, I can be very persuasive."

I straightened up, tipped my cup toward me to see if there was anything left in it and then decided I'd rather have coffee than half a cup of cold tea. I got to my feet and started collecting the cups and spoons. "We got so focused on the driver you didn't finish telling me what you learned at the library," I said.

Rose picked up the tray she'd used to bring everything downstairs and handed it to me.

"The library board was having their meeting, which

we also knew," she said. "It got a little . . . contentious. Stella and Vincent had words and she stormed out."

"Over how to spend the money they're getting."

Rose sighed. "Yes. I talked to a couple of people, and I think it's fair to say the argument had turned into more than just a difference of opinion on spending some money. Stella called Swift a bully and he said she was inflexible. He did go after her and try to get her to come back."

"You don't think he was completely wrong."

Rose hesitated before she answered. "I think that the two of them had butted heads on so many issues they had both lost perspective."

"Such a dramatic argument doesn't help Stella's case."

"No, it doesn't," Rose said. "Which is why we have to figure out as fast as we can who really killed Vincent."

I nodded. "So what else was going on at the library besides the board meeting?"

"There was also a meeting of an organization that promotes organ donation."

"Madison Telfer's parents," I said. I picked up the tray and we headed for the shop.

Rose nodded. "I had the same thought. I have no idea if they were actually there, but it shouldn't be that difficult to find out. Aside from those two meetings, there were several tutors working with students from Horizons, the literacy program, plus the usual patrons borrowing books and magazines and using the computers and the study carrels."

"That's a lot more people than I expected for a Monday night."

Rose leaned over and picked a bit of cat hair from my sleeve. I had no idea where Elvis was; probably out in the workroom with Avery. "The library is a busy spot," she said as she straightened up. "There are fewer and fewer places to have meetings or run a program that don't charge for the space. And the library is somewhere to be around other people even if you don't talk to anyone. I know Teresa spends a lot of time there."

Teresa Reynard was a very solitary person. I suspected she fell somewhere on the autism spectrum. I wasn't surprised she liked the library. She'd told me once that she liked books, that they were a lot more predictable than people.

"So how are we going to sort through all those people?" I said to Rose. "We're never going to be able to find and talk to them all."

"I think we just have to make a list of suspects and see if any of those names were at the library Monday night."

"I can't think of a better plan," I said. "I need to check the website orders. Can we talk about that list on the way home? And I still haven't told you what I learned from Josh."

Rose smiled. "Alfred should be in on both of those conversations. Everything can wait until then."

Liz came to get Avery at the end of the day. She wore black wool trousers and a bulky sweater, also black, with a cardinal red quilted vest. I was wearing paint-speckled jeans and an equally paint-spattered plaid flannel shirt with a hole in the left elbow. I sometimes had the feeling that Liz could step outside in the middle of a blizzard and the snow would somehow fall around her and not on her.

I held my arms out to my sides and leaned in to kiss her cheek.

"What's that for?" she said.

"For being you. For hiring Jane."

"She said you were trying to find Vincent's driver."

I nodded. "Thanks to Jane, we've already talked to him."

"I talked to Channing," Liz said, pulling off her gloves. "He says the settlement with Vincent and Jacob Pena was in the realm of more than half a million dollars each."

"That's half a million reasons for someone to want Vincent dead," I said, hoping that neither Brent LeBlanc nor Earle Weyman was that someone.

"Channing also mentioned that rumor has it—and he emphasized it was just a rumor—Vincent was going to cut his son out of his will."

"*Was* going to cut him out or *had* cut him out?"

Liz tapped a temple with one finger. "Great minds think alike," she said. "I asked the same question; Channing said he'd heard was going to—in other words, Vincent might have been giving his son one last chance to come back to North Harbor and work with him."

"I wonder if William took it," I said.

Liz raised one perfectly arched eyebrow. "That's the million-dollar question."

Mr. P. got back about four o'clock with a cat-that-swallowed-the-canary look about him. Or maybe an

Elvis-that-swallowed-a-sardine look would have been a better description. As we pulled out of the parking lot at the end of the day, I gave him and Rose a brief rundown on what Josh had told me about the lawsuit against the state and how Earle Weyman and Brent LeBlanc had lost their jobs.

"I can't believe Brent would kill anyone," Rose said. "He was a dear child, but he struggled a bit with reading. It wasn't that he had a reading disability per se; it was more that he didn't get the help he needed at home. He was the oldest of seven kids and he spent more time with the younger ones than he did on his schoolwork. In some ways he was like a little adult, not like a child at all. Too many responsibilities."

"We need to talk to him, Rosie," Mr. P. said gently.

Rose nodded. "I know. I should be able to find out where he is."

"Cleveland will be stopping by in the next couple of days," I said. "I'll talk to him about Earle. I admit I have problems believing either Earle or Brent could be the killer. It's a long time to hold a grudge."

"Sometimes things fester," Mr. P. said from the backseat. "I don't think we can eliminate either man, not yet."

I nodded, keeping my eyes on the road. "And I think Madison Telfer's father needs to be on our list as well."

"What about his wife?" Rose asked.

"According to Josh, she wasn't holding a grudge. She forgave Jacob."

"I still think we should talk to her," Rose said. "She's Madison's mother."

"Why don't we start with Mr. Telfer?" Mr. P. said. "I'll call his office in the morning and make an appointment."

"All right," I said. Out of the corner of my eye I saw Rose nodding. I stopped to let a man walking three small, furry dogs cross the street. "Did you learn anything at the courthouse?" I asked Mr. P. I glanced in the rearview mirror in time to see him smile.

"I did," he said. "William Swift changed his name to William Reeves."

"That should make him easier to find," Rose said.

"'Reeves' was the young man's mother's name. I suspected it might be what he'd chosen. His issues were with his father. Using Reeves keeps him connected to his mother's side of the family."

"Do you think he'll show up for the funeral?" I asked. "I'm assuming there will be some kind of service."

"I expect so," Rose said. "If William does come, it will make our job a little easier." I heard her rummaging in the tote bag at her feet.

"Are you looking for the list Liz sent you?"

"It's all right. I have it," she said. "We can cross off the first name. He's in Costa Rica having a secret facelift."

"If it's secret, how do you know?" I asked. I shot a quick look in her direction again.

She smiled an enigmatic smile and patted her hair. "I'm a sweet little old lady, and people just like to tell me things."

I gave a snort of laughter. "In other words, people

seriously underestimate you and you have the inter-rogation skills of a Cold War CIA agent."

"You could put it that way," she said, "but my way sounds nicer."

She half turned in her seat and I realized she was showing the list to Mr. P. "Didn't he break his hand?"

"Chopping ice off his steps with a meat mallet."

They eliminated a third name because Rose said the woman wore heels higher than Liz did. "There's no way she could have gotten away from the crime scene quickly and without being heard."

By that point we had pulled into the driveway. I turned to look at Rose. "Who are we left with?" I asked.

"Aside from Brent and Earle and Mr. Telfer, Neill Halloran."

I shook my head. "Absolutely not. Judge Halloran couldn't kill anyone."

"No, he couldn't," Mr. P. said. "Not deliberately. But Vincent Swift's murder looks like something that happened spur-of-the-moment. Neill Halloran could have done it. Anyone could have done it."

"I don't think so," I said, realizing I sounded like a petulant child. "You couldn't have. No matter what the provocation."

"Even me, Sarah," he said.

I took a breath and let it out. "We're going to have to agree to disagree on this one."

Rose invited me for supper. I thanked her but turned down the invitation. I had some of Charlotte's chicken soup in my refrigerator. After supper I looked up Damian Telfer on my computer while Elvis sprawled across my legs and did his best to get in the way. I found a couple of photos of the Telfers walking into the courthouse for Jacob Pena's sentencing. Damian had dark hair and brown eyes and his face was guarded, closed off. Natalie Telfer clutched her husband's hand tightly. She was small and thin; the navy coat she wore hung loosely from her shoulders. She had chin-length blond hair that covered part of her face; even so, I could see her grief in the way she stood, her body folded in on itself.

Studying the photograph I realized I knew Natalie. Not well, but well enough to smile, say hello and have a brief conversation. She was a runner, too. We'd been in several of the same road races and I saw her out training from time to time.

Damian Telfer and Vincent Swift had worked for the same financial firm at one time, I learned. Damian had also been involved with keeping the Sunflower Window in town, which meant Gram and Liz likely knew him. And as a teenager he had worked as a counselor at the Sunshine Camp—the summer camp run by the Emmerson Foundation.

I called Liz.

"What's up, toots?" she said.

"Damian Telfer was on your list of people who had issues with Vincent Swift. I'm assuming you remember him from when he was a camp counselor."

"Of course I do. I'm not that far gone yet."

"What's he like?' I asked.

"He was good with the kids," she said. "He'd make them feel they could do whatever they set their mind to. He helped them believe in themselves—not the kind of thing you see often in a sixteen-year-old."

"Were there any problems?"

"Well, he didn't bean anyone with a crystal ball," Liz said, "if that's what you're asking."

"It wasn't exactly what I meant," I said.

"He did get into a scuffle with another counselor he thought was bullying some of the campers."

"Was he right?"

"He was. Something you should know about Damian: He had—and likely still has—a strong sense of right and wrong."

I knew that Liz could also be a pretty black-and-white person. "So you don't necessarily think that's a bad thing."

"I think if you don't stand for something, you'll fall for anything."

"He was part of the Sunflower Window project as well."

"An important part. He made sure all the checks and balances were in place to safeguard the money that was being donated."

Elvis worked his way up onto my lap and started washing his face. "What do you know about his skills as a financial adviser?"

"According to everything I've heard, Damian's clients like him. He's somewhat conservative, but his clients are older and that works for them."

"That's good to know," I said.

"Are you planning on talking to Damian?" Liz asked.

"Mr. P. is going to make an appointment."

"No, no," she said and I could picture her shaking her head. "I'll call Alfred. I should be the one to see Damian. He knows me. He'll talk to me."

"Do I get to come with you?"

Liz gave a sigh. "If I say no, will that dissuade you?"

"C'mon," I wheedled. "You need me. We're Cagney and Lacey, Nancy Drew and George, Trixie Belden and Honey Wheeler, Rocky and Bullwinkle."

"We're a moose and a flying squirrel?" Liz said drily.

"We're a team." I slid down so I was mostly sitting on my tailbone and stretched out my legs, which got me a glare from Elvis, who was still doing his cat beauty routine.

"Fine, you can come. I'll let you know tomorrow what time. Don't dress like you have no money. You don't know who else we might talk to besides Damian."

The very first time Liz and I had gone on a fact-finding mission, she'd told me to wear something that exposed some leg. This, at least, was an improvement over those instructions.

"I don't have any money," I said.

"Number one, you don't need to advertise that. Number two, it never hurts to use all the tools in your toolbox."

"We're going to ask Damian Telfer a few questions. The only tool I need is between my ears."

"It's adorable that you actually believe that," she said. "I'll talk to you in the morning. I'm serious about the clothes. Don't dress like a hippie."

She hung up before I could ask what not dressing like a hippie looked like.

Chapter 13

Rose was waiting for me in the hallway in the morning, wearing her quilted jacket and a red-and-gray-striped scarf. She was carrying one of her tote bags and I was pretty sure I could smell cinnamon, which I was hoping meant she had a coffee cake in the bag.

"It seems our plans have changed," she said, glancing at the garment bag I was carrying.

Either Liz had called her or Mr. P. had. "I'm sorry," I said. "I called Liz for information after I found out that Damian Telfer had been a counselor at the Sunshine Camp. I didn't realize she'd take over going to see him." Although I probably should have, I knew.

Rose waved away my apology with her free hand. "It's all right. Liz probably *is* the better choice for this interview." Her gaze narrowed. "And if you tell her that, it will be a very long time before you eat another of my cherry coffee cakes."

I smiled. "You play hardball."

She cocked an eyebrow at me. "I'm more than just a cute little piece of fluff, you know."

Mac was out in the workshop when we pulled into the parking lot at Second Chance. He walked over as we got out of the car. He was smiling. "I got the mantel," he said, "and for five dollars less than the seller was asking. And I spent five dollars for a brass plant stand."

Rose and I walked over to the old garage to take a look. The plant stand was dull and black with tarnish, although the sleek, curved leg design was pretty. Rose set her bag down, walked all the way around the stand, then reached up and patted Mac's cheek, "It's all right. No one is going to go broke over five dollars." She picked up her tote bag and started for the shop. "I'm going to put on the kettle," she said.

Mac looked at me. "What do you think?"

"I really want to believe it was a good deal," I said, "but it's hard not to side with Rose."

"Oh ye of little faith," he said. "It's just grime and tarnish. A good cleaning with some baking soda and lemon juice and you—and Rose—will be eating your words."

I looked at the mantel, which he had propped against the wall.

"You were right about the duct tape, unfortunately."

I scraped at one edge with a fingernail. "I think a hair dryer will help get it off." I bent down for a closer look at the design on the front. "The carved detail is even better than I had hoped. I think it was well worth what you paid."

Mac rubbed his hand over the top of his head. "I

still find it hard to believe those mantels are so popular. When you said people are buying them to put in a room to create the illusion of a fireplace just for the cozy feeling, I thought you were—"

"—not as right as I usually am?" I teased.

He grinned. "Pretty much," he said.

"Are you going to be around all day?" I asked as we started for the shop.

"I need to get some sandpaper, but I can do that anytime. What do you need?"

I indicated the garment bag. "Sometime today, I hope, I'm going with Liz to talk to Damian Telfer."

"Why Liz?" Mac asked.

"Because Damian Telfer worked at the Sunshine Camp when he was a teenager."

"So she knows him."

I nodded. "And likes him." I blew out a breath. "Am I wrong to want Vincent Swift's murder to be just some random act of violence by a total stranger? I don't like the idea of Mr. Telfer being the killer any more than I like the thought of it being Stella or Earle Weyman or anyone else I know."

I had crumpled the garment bag without even realizing it. Mac took it from my hand and gave it a shake before draping it over his shoulder. "You're not wrong," he said, "but I'm not so sure it's going to work out the way you want it to."

Liz called about half an hour later just as I was getting ready to put a second coat of paint on the chairs. The tan paint had turned out to be a good color choice. "Our appointment is for eleven," she said.

"Okay, Bullwinkle, I'll be ready," I said.

"You can be replaced with a self-driving car," Liz retorted.

"It wouldn't have my winning personality." I was still laughing when she hung up on me.

A tour bus pulled into the parking lot just as I had finished painting the back of one of the chairs. More than two dozen people crowded into the shop. We sold a lot of small things—vases, tablecloths, three pairs of candleholders, the last of the teddy bears and so many teacups I lost count.

I had to hustle to get ready for Liz so she was waiting when I came downstairs wearing a black pencil skirt with a fitted white shirt.

"Wow!" Mac said.

I felt my cheeks redden.

Liz, who looked perfect, as always, in a cranberry three-quarter-length coat over a chocolate-colored skirt, nodded her approval and said, "You clean up well for a flying squirrel."

Mac helped me put on my coat. "Flying squirrel?" he whispered.

"I'll tell you later," I said.

Liz gave me directions and handed over her keys.

"I see you didn't go for the self-driving car," I teased.

"And I see *you* are still saucy."

"Does Damian know why we're coming to see him?" I asked as we pulled out of the parking lot.

"Of course not," Liz said. "This isn't my debutante

ball. I know my way around, and I know we don't want to hear any rehearsed answers."

"How did you get the appointment then?"

"I called Damian's assistant." I glanced sideways at her. "I'm Elizabeth Emmerson Kiley French. I don't generally have trouble getting appointments."

I looked at the road again. "I want to be you when I grow up," I said. Out of the corner of my eye I saw her smile.

"Well, of course you do," she said.

Damian Telfer's office was on the second floor of the old North Harbor Bank building, a stone structure that would probably still be standing when many of the newer buildings in North Harbor were gone. I had a vivid memory of Mom and Gram bringing me into the bank to opening my very first savings account. My favorite part had been the cherry sucker the teller gave me.

The bank's original marble floors and embellished ceilings had been restored and everything was understated, tasteful and just a little intimidating, which was probably exactly the effect the investment firm had been going for.

Liz, of course, walked in like she owned the place. She could be a little intimidating, too. The receptionist, a young man of maybe twenty-five, smiled as she approached. "Hello, Mrs. French," he said. "It's a pleasure to see you. Mr. Telfer is expecting you; please, come this way."

"Thank you," Liz replied, all graciousness in return. Being recognized always scored points with her.

As she'd once told a receptionist who had no clue who she was, "You should know who the movers and shakers are in this town."

Damian Telfer smiled when he caught sight of Liz—a genuine smile, not one out of politeness or professionalism. He came around his chrome and glass desk and took her hand in both of his. "Liz, it's so good to see you," he said.

"It's good to see you as well, Damian," Liz said. I could tell from the look in her eyes that she was genuinely pleased to be there, despite the reason for our visit.

"Thank you for this year's contribution to Madison's scholarship fund," he said. "It was very generous of you."

"It's a wonderful memorial. I'm happy to make a donation."

I hadn't known that Liz had been contributing to a scholarship in Madison Telfer's memory, but I shouldn't have been surprised. She was always happy to tell anyone what the foundation that carried her family name was up to, but she was a lot more circumspect about the good deeds she did herself.

She turned to me then. "Damian, this is my friend Sarah Grayson. Isabel is her grandmother."

We shook hands. He had a decent handshake, firm without giving the feeling that he was trying to squeeze my hand as though juicing a lemon. A long scar traced across the back of his hand to just above his wrist.

"The Sunflower Window wouldn't be staying in

town if it wasn't for your grandmother and Liz," he said. "They put in a lot of work."

"I've heard that you did as well," I said.

"I just pushed paper around," he said. "But I'm glad it helped."

Damian Telfer looked like the photos I'd seen of him online. His dark hair was a bit longer than it had been in the pictures, combed straight back from his face, and there was a snow-white streak in it on the right-hand side. His eyes, I realized, were hazel, not brown.

Damian indicated the two chrome and leather chairs in front of his desk. We sat down and he turned his attention to Liz.

"What can I do for you?" he asked.

"You obviously know about Vincent Swift's death," she said, crossing one leg over the other and folding her hands in her lap.

The muscles along his jawline tightened. "I do and I doubt that you, of all people, are here soliciting for a memorial tribute."

The expression on Liz's face didn't change. "No, I'm not." She glanced in my direction for a moment. "Stella Hall is my friend. The police have been questioning her."

"If she killed Vincent, I'll be happy to contribute to a defense fund," Damian said.

"She didn't," Liz said. "And I don't want to see her get railroaded."

"So you came to ask me if I killed him."

Her face softened. "You had a reason to, if anyone

did. I don't want to see you sandbagged for something I know you wouldn't do."

Damian looked away, out the window to the left of his desk. "I didn't do it," he said, "but there were times over the last two-and-a-half years that I thought about killing the man." I could hear the pain in the brittleness of his voice. "I can't pretend I'm sorry that Vincent Swift is dead. Good riddance, as far as I'm concerned."

"No one would fault you for feeling that way," Liz said.

His gaze shifted back to us again. "My dislike of Vincent goes back to before Madison died, Liz. He worked here at one time, and I didn't like the way he did business. I didn't trust him."

"What do you mean?" I asked.

"More than once Vincent had a hunch about a stock that then took off and made money for his clients. On one occasion he just had a feeling a business was going to have problems with the EPA. All his clients dumped their shares in time. All of them."

"You thought he was somehow using inside information."

Damian nodded. "I was certain of it. I still am. You can look at trends in the economy and in popular culture. You can pay attention to Congress, the European Union and crops in Costa Rica, for that matter—I've done all of those things—and you still can't always predict what the market will do, let alone what will happen to one particular stock."

"I take it you couldn't prove your suspicions," Liz said.

His right hand tightened into a fist, his knuckles stretching the skin so tightly I thought it would tear along the scar. Damian didn't seem to notice. "I was working on that when the accident happened. Then, while we were trying to find a way to put our lives back together again, I discovered Vincent was trying to poach my clients. He claimed he just wanted to be helpful, but I didn't buy that for a second."

His voice had risen with each word and now he took a couple of slow, deep breaths. "Everything he touched got tainted," he said, his voice under control again. He seemed to see his hand for the first time and he unclenched it and picked up a pen that was lying on the desk in front of him. "The man paid for one of the best criminal defense lawyers on the East Coast for Jacob Pena. Jacob killed my daughter and ended up getting money for it when Vincent brought that lawsuit against the state. He put the blame on good, hardworking men; and that kid, whose own parents had taken away the keys to their car because he'd been caught speeding, was handed hundreds of thousands of dollars. Where is the justice in that?"

I could see the anguish in his eyes and the anger as well.

Liz cleared her throat. "You don't blame the road crew," she said.

Damian shook his head. He looked down at the top of his desk. "It wasn't their fault," he said. After a moment he looked up again. "Yes, they had a schedule they were supposed to follow, but they were just a few minutes behind. And that could have been because they were a few minutes late leaving the diner, or it could have been because of traffic, or maybe they slowed down for a snow squall that temporarily impaired their visibility. What caused the accident was Jacob's reckless driving."

He swiped a hand over his mouth. "There was a nurse in the car right behind them on the road. She told the police that she didn't know exactly how fast she was going, but she generally drove a bit below the speed limit if it was snowing and it was that night. She said the SUV was in front of her and it was pulling away. In the civil trial Vincent's lawyers made it seem like the nurse was going a fair bit below the speed limit, which meant Jacob was driving at the limit. Vincent said he couldn't remember the drive at all, but Jacob knew nothing would happen if he was caught speeding. Nothing more than the equivalent of a slap on the wrist had happened the first time, thanks to his godfather. He thought the rules didn't apply to him, and I don't think that Vincent and Madison being in the vehicle would have made any difference. Fact of the matter is, the kid just shouldn't have been behind the wheel at all, and that's on Vincent."

Liz leaned forward and put her hand on Damian's for a moment. "How does Natalie feel about all of this?" she asked.

Damian almost smiled at the mention of his wife's name. "She's a much better person than I am. She didn't kill Vincent, that's for sure. The idea of hurting another living thing . . ." He shook his head. "Her brother has a cottage. There were bats up in the attic. James just wanted to put some poison down and get rid of them. Natalie was horrified. She kept at James until he agreed to have an exterminator remove the bats and release them somewhere else, and then she went out to make sure the company he hired actually did it."

Liz smiled and leaned back in her seat again. "That sounds like Natalie."

"She believes that knowing he caused Madison's death is enough punishment for Jacob. I don't have that kind of forgiveness in me."

Liz's smile faded. "I understand that," she said. She locked eyes with Damian. Something passed between them and I had the sense that Liz really did understand how he felt. She wasn't just saying the words.

For a long moment neither one of them spoke. "I'm glad he's dead," Damian finally said.

Liz nodded. "I understand that, too." She paused. "Where were you Monday night? And is there anyone who can verify that—other than Natalie, if possible. The police will be asking."

He twisted the pen and set it spinning on the desktop. "For part of the time I was at the library. Lots of people saw me."

I saw Liz stiffen. "What were you doing at the library?" she asked.

"There was an event celebrating and promoting organ donation. Madison's heart and her lungs went to two people and her corneas to two others." He swallowed and pressed his lips together for a moment. "I know she would have liked that," he continued, his voice raspy now, "and I'm glad that people get another chance at life because of her. I'm even happy that some part of her lives on. But I can't watch it. That part is just too much."

I felt my chest tighten. His grief was so raw. "Natalie stayed. I called a ride and went home."

He reached into his pocket and pulled out his cell phone. He swiped a finger across the screen several times and then held the phone out so Liz and I could see it. I noted the time he'd made the call. Damian would have been home long before Jess and I left The Black Bear and before Vincent Swift left the library. I felt a rush of relief.

"I won't dance on Vincent Swift's grave but I won't pretend I'm sorry, either," he said.

"You won't be the only one who feels that way," Liz said. She glanced at me and her eyes narrowed slightly.

I gave an almost imperceptible nod. Damian wasn't our killer. We didn't need to know anything else.

Liz got to her feet and I did the same. "Thank you for talking to us," she said. "If the police want to talk to you—" She stopped. "*When* the police want to talk to you, take a lawyer with you. And if you need anything—anything at all—I expect you to call me."

Damian smiled. "Good to have you in my corner."

She smiled back at him. "Always. Tell Natalie I'm thinking about her."

"I will," he said. He turned his attention to me. "Please give Isabel my best."

"I'll do that," I said.

Liz and I stepped into the elevator to take us down to the main floor. When the door closed I laid my head on her shoulder. "I love you, Elizabeth Emmerson Kiley French," I said.

"And what's that for?" she asked.

"It seems to me that Vincent Swift used his money and his family name to bully people, while you use yours to do good things like donate to Madison Telfer's scholarship fund."

"Madison was a lovely girl," she said softly. "You would have liked her."

"You did, so I know I would have."

She smiled.

"How did Damian get the scar on the back of his hand?" I asked.

"You noticed that."

I nodded.

Liz sighed. "After the state lost the civil lawsuit, he punched a wall at the courthouse and broke his hand. He had to have surgery."

"I'm surprised I didn't see anything about that in the news coverage."

She shrugged. "There were only a few people around at the time and they all decided it wasn't worth writing about." I had a feeling I knew who had helped those people make that decision.

"I'm glad Damian has an alibi," I said, "because I don't think I'd be able to turn him in if he were guilty." I lifted my head and looked at Liz. "What does that make me?"

Liz patted my cheek. "Human," she said.

Chapter 14

I drove Liz's car back to the shop. "Are you coming in?" I asked as I pulled into the parking lot.

She checked her watch. "Not right now. I have places to go and people to see," she said. "I'll be back to pick up Avery."

I climbed out of the driver's seat and Liz walked around to take my place. "You really aren't sorry he's dead, are you?" I said.

She shook her head. "Not in the slightest. I'm not saying he deserved to be hit over the head and left to die in the street. I don't condone murder. But Vincent Swift could have made the world a better place and he chose—*chose*—not to do that. His death does not diminish me at all."

Mr. P. was on his phone when I poked my head into his office. He held up one finger so I waited, unzippering my jacket, slipping it off and folding it over my arm.

"Thank you," he said to the person on the other

end of the line. "I appreciate your help." He ended the call and set his cell phone down on the desk. He smiled at me. "How did your visit with Mr. Telfer go?"

"It's not him," I said. I explained about the ride-share and the call log.

"For Mr. Telfer's sake, I'm happy to hear that," Mr. P. said.

"But it doesn't do Stella any good."

He shook his head. "No, it doesn't."

The rest of the day was busy. I finished painting the chairs and Avery and I packed the *National Geographics* to go to our very happy collector. I spent a few minutes on my laptop reading Vincent Swift's obituary. It contained very little information about his early life, but I did learn that he had been a day student at a small private school called Camden Collegiate. It seemed like a good place to start looking into lost loves and roads not taken.

Rose had already gone home, and Charlotte left at the end of the day with Liz and Avery. Mr. P. and Mac headed out shortly after. They were driving to Rockport to look at, and possibly buy, a bed frame and dresser for the old man.

"You two have fun. Don't get too rowdy," I told Mr. P. as he wound a scarf around his neck.

"I make no promises I may not be able to keep," he said solemnly.

"Looks like it's just you and me," I said to Elvis as I put on my boots. He was sitting in the middle of my desk. He cocked his furry black head to one side and studied me for a moment. Then he made a sound a lot like a sigh.

I gave Elvis his supper, had a quick shower and changed. I set the timer on the TV so he wouldn't miss *Jeopardy!* and headed down to meet Jess. As usual she had gotten to the pub first and gotten us a good table.

"Is Nick joining us?" she asked. She was wearing black leggings, low black boots and a cowl-necked purple sweater.

"As far as I know," I said, slipping out of my jacket and hanging it on the back of my chair. "And could we not talk about the case when he gets here?"

"Any leads so far?"

"More questions than answers at this point. The list of people who didn't like Vincent Swift is a long one."

She tucked her hair behind one ear. "That's sad. I'd hate to think I'd get to the end of my life and my enemies would outnumber my friends."

"That could never happen to you," I said. There was a menu on the table and I picked it up even though I pretty much knew what I was going to order.

"What could never happen to Jess?" Nick's voice said from behind me

"I said I'd hate to die with more enemies than friends," she said. "We were talking about Mr. Swift."

"I don't think you have to worry about that," he said. He shrugged out of his jacket, draped it over the back of the chair next to me and sat down.

"So have you figured out who killed the old man

yet?" Jess asked in the same tone of voice she might have used to ask him what he was going to order.

I set the menu down and glared at Jess. "What happened to 'could we not talk about the case'?"

"I like Stella," she said.

"And what? I don't?" Nick retorted.

I gave him a look. "Nobody said that."

"I have a job to do," he said, an edge of testiness in his voice. "And I can't do it properly if I let my personal feelings get in the way."

I looked around for a server. I needed food and it seemed to me that Nick was probably hungry, too.

"You didn't answer my question," Jess said, in the same conversational tone she'd used before. She was sitting sideways in her chair, one leg crossed over the other, her foot bobbing up and down.

"It's not my job to find the person who killed Vincent Swift." Nick seemed to bite the end off all his words. "It's my job to collect evidence for the medical examiner's office."

Jess shrugged. "Okay. And did any of this evidence point to a suspect? I mean other than Stella."

Jess had been around the edges of the Angels' cases in the past but this was the first time she'd been involved in one. Because she'd seen Vincent Swift lying on the ground, because she'd called 911 and taken care of Stella, I think it all felt very personal to her.

Nick pulled a hand down over his chin. "Look, I get that you and Sarah stumbled on the crime scene and that you feel protective about Stella, but no one is treating her like a criminal."

"Really?" Jess said. "Because I was there and it sure

looked that way to me. She's an older woman; it was cold Monday night, Nick. Freezing. And the officer who showed up didn't offer to let her sit in his cruiser. He didn't even offer a blanket and *don't* tell me he didn't have such a thing because my shop was one of the drop-off spots last year when they were collecting blankets so every police car could have a couple in their trunk." I noticed that she'd left out the fact that when Michele arrived and offered to let Stella wait in the cruiser, Stella had refused. And so had Jess.

"That shouldn't have happened," Nick said.

I slapped my hand down hard on the table. Nick jumped and so did Jess. I had made a satisfyingly loud noise, loud enough that the people at the next table turned to look. I smiled and nodded reassuringly when what I really wanted to do was rub my palm because not only was slapping the table loud, it also made my hand sting like crazy.

"Knock it off! Both of you!" I said. "Or I'm taking my chair and going to sit over there with Glenn and whoever the heck is with him." I jerked my head in the general direction of where Glenn McNamara and his friends were sitting.

"I'm sorry," Jess said. She did look contrite. "I just . . . I just don't want anyone to think Stella could have done this just because the police are treating her like she's a suspect."

"Nobody is treating her like a suspect," Nick said.

I got to my feet and moved to pick up my chair. Jess immediately stretched an arm across the table. "No more case talk, Sarah. I promise."

Nick grabbed the side of my chair. "I'm sorry, too." He looked at Jess. "Truce?"

She nodded. "Truce."

Nick let go of my chair.

I set it back on the floor and sat down again. "Could you flag down a server, please?" I said to Jess. "I'd like to order before Sam and the boys come out."

"Me, too," Nick said. "And I'm buying." He cocked an eyebrow at Jess. "Chips and salsa?"

"You think you can buy your way back onto my A list with chips and salsa?" she asked. Just a trace of a teasing smile played across her face.

"Well, not with a medium order, but maybe the large."

Jess laughed. "So order me the large and see what happens." She looked around, spotted a server even though I still couldn't see one and raised her hand.

"How does she do that?" Nick said to me as a young man approached our table.

"If you know how the magic trick is done, it ruins the fun," I said.

Nick and I both chose the Bear Burger, which was Sam's take on a cheeseburger, made with fresh mozzarella cheese, a heap of fried onions and a spicy mayo-mustard blend that was Sam's own creation. And Nick added a large order of tortilla chips and salsa for Jess.

"Hey, I have a new bride," Jess said once the server had gone to take our orders to the kitchen. Jess's reputation for creating beautiful wedding dresses was spreading beyond North Harbor

"When's the wedding?" I asked, happy to be talking about anything other than the Swift case.

"May," Jess said.

"Spring bride," I said. North Harbor was beautiful that time of year. "It doesn't give you much time, though."

She nodded. "I know, but I just couldn't say no to this bride." She pulled out her phone, scrolled until she found what she was looking for and then held the phone out to Nick and me. On the screen was a beaming white-haired woman holding out her left hand to show off the beautiful diamond ring on her finger. "Her name is Avis. She's eighty-six. The groom is eighty-two."

"She looks so happy," I said.

Jess smiled. "She is. She can't stop smiling. She told me she's waited seventy years to marry this man."

"That's so romantic."

"Little bit less so when you find out she's already had three husbands."

"You go, Avis," Nick said.

I swatted him with the back of my hand and he smirked at me.

At the same time I saw our server coming in our direction balancing a large tray of food while Sam and the boys headed for the small stage. At least for now all was right with my world.

As usual the band was great, and I was sorry when Sam thanked everyone for coming and said, "Come back next week."

"There's someone I need to talk to," Jess said. "I won't be very long."

"Go ahead," I said. Across the room Sam was surrounded by people. He spotted me and smiled. I smiled back and put a hand to my chest for a moment, my way of saying, "Love you."

He nodded.

Next to me Nick pulled out his phone, checked the screen and then shoved it back in his pocket again.

"Everything okay?" I asked.

He nodded. "Surprisingly, yes." He cleared his throat. "I'm really sorry. I shouldn't have gotten into it with Jess. I know it had to have been hard for her to see Swift's body, to go through what happened Monday night. I know she's worried about Stella. She's not the only one. I don't want this case or any case to come between us."

"It won't," I said.

"Didn't it hurt when you smacked the table like that?"

I laughed. "Yeah, it really did, but I didn't want either one of you to know that because it would ruin the effect of my dramatic gesture."

"So do Rose and Mr. P. have any leads?"

"Not yet," I said. "Do the police?"

He shook his head. "Not yet, as far as I know."

"Is that good?"

Nick shrugged. "I'm not sure."

I glanced over at the empty stage. "So when are you going to sit in with the guys again?"

He ran a hand through his hair. "I don't know. I haven't had much time lately to pick up a guitar." His eyes narrowed when I didn't say anything. "Are you going to tell me I need to stop working so much and get a life?"

"You mean you're not sick of hearing me say that?"

He smiled. "What about you? When was the last time you played?"

I shrugged. "I don't know. A while ago." My guitar had belonged to my father—my biological father. Every time I took it out it stirred up some uncomfortable feelings that I didn't want to deal with.

"Maybe we should make a New Year's resolution. I'll work on getting some balance in my life and you'll start playing again."

"You're supposed to make New Year's resolutions at the beginning of January, not the end," I said lightly.

"I don't think the New Year's police will come after us," Nick said. He hesitated. "It's a beautiful guitar, Sarah. It should be played."

I knew he was right. Then Jess came back, which saved me from having to say anything.

Elvis and I pulled into the parking lot at the shop the next morning just as Mr. P. came along the sidewalk. Rose had the morning off. Elvis looked out the window and meowed loudly.

"Yes, I see him," I said. I grabbed my messenger bag and climbed out of the SUV.

Elvis looked expectantly at me.

I shook my head. "Number one, I am not Rose. Number two, you are perfectly capable of walking to the back door."

He didn't so much as twitch a whisker.

"Fine," I said. "You can stay out here all morning."

His response was to stretch out on the seat, tucking in his two front paws as though he was prepared to stay out there in the cold. A cat had called my bluff.

I scooped him up with my free arm. He licked my chin and there was a self-satisfied gleam in his green eyes. "You don't have to be so smug," I said.

Mr. P. came across the lot to join us. "Good morning, Elvis. Good morning, Sarah," he said. He looked like a six year-old who had been dressed by an overprotective grandmother. He wore a hooded parka with one of Rose's knitted hats and a pair of earmuffs. A long scarf was wound around his neck. His pant legs were tucked into a pair of Bean boots very similar to Avery's and he had thick fleece gloves for his hands.

He held up one hand. "I know what you're going to say. You would have been happy to pick me up, and I appreciate the thought, but a brisk walk on a morning like this keeps me young."

Our breath hung in the air like puffs of smoke.

"It keeps you young because it's like you've been cryogenically preserved," I said as we started for the back door.

"At one time I considered doing that after my demise," Mr. P. said.

"What made you change your mind?"

"Primarily, the fact that all the people I cared about would be gone. And strawberries."

I frowned. "Strawberries?"

"Yes. You know how delicious fresh strawberries are when they're in season."

"As someone who has eaten Rose's strawberry shortcake many, many times, yes I do."

Mr. P. smiled. "And you know Rosie always freezes some berries."

"So we can have them over the holidays." I fished my keys out of my pocket. Mr. P. took Elvis from me and I unlocked the back door.

"And are they good?" he asked, setting the cat on the floor.

I nodded. "Yes, they are." I felt the conversation had gotten a long way from it being a cold walk for him this morning.

"Are they the same as fresh?"

I thought about all the times I'd helped Rose with her strawberry shortcake, cutting the plumb, juicy berries and sprinkling them with sugar. "No," I said.

He took off his glasses, which had steamed up in the warmth of the workroom. "That's the other reason. I was concerned that if I was brought back to life the thawed version of me wouldn't be the same as the fresh one had been."

He pulled out his own keys and unlocked the door to the Angels' office. "Do you have a few minutes?" he asked. "I discovered some interesting information about Damian Telfer last night."

"Just let me get rid of these things in my office and grab a cup of coffee," I said. "Would you like a cup? Or I could make the tea?"

"I think I'll have coffee as well," he said.

I nodded. "I'll be right back."

Mac was just coming down the stairs. "Good

morning," he said with a smile. "How was the jam?"
He and Mr. P. had gotten back late and I hadn't talked
to him after I'd gotten home.

"Sam did a couple of Bob Seeger songs," I said,
smiling at the memory. "It was great."

Elvis wandered in, meowed a "hello" at Mac and
headed past him up the stairs.

"I forgot to ask Mr. P. Did you buy the bed frame?"

He nodded. "And the dresser. Solid wood, dove-
tailed joints, and the price was ridiculously low."

I knew what that meant. "And the catch is?"

"Both pieces need refinishing."

"So you have a new project," I teased.

He gave me a slightly embarrassed smile. "I have a
new project. But I don't mind, and Avery will help."

"So will I," I said. "But right now I need to dump
everything in my office. Mr. P. says he has some new
information about Damian Telfer."

"Good or bad?" Mac asked.

I shrugged. "I don't know yet."

I put my coat and my messenger bag in my office
and changed my boots for shoes. Then I got coffee for
Mr. P. and myself and went back down to the sunporch.

"Thank you, my dear," he said as I handed him one
of the two mugs I was carrying.

"So what did you find out?" I asked.

He took a sip from his coffee and gave a small nod
of approval. "First of all, I learned that Mr. Telfer had
an assault charge in his past."

"How far in his past?"

"Ten years ago. He went after a man who was beating a dog. When the man told him it was none of his business—in far more crude language from what I read—Mr. Telfer shoved him."

I took a sip of my own coffee. "I know it's wrong to take the law into your own hands, but beating an animal, that's a lot worse."

"I agree," Mr. P. said.

"There's something else, isn't there?" I said.

He nodded. "I'm afraid there is and it's far more troubling than punching a bully in the nose. I checked Mr. Telfer's alibi."

"You mean the rideshare?"

"Yes."

My chest tightened. "Did his ride not show up? Did he cancel?"

"No." He shook his head. "But he didn't go home the way he said he did. He had the driver let him off just a few blocks away from where he got picked up."

"Maybe he forgot something," I said. Damian Telfer couldn't have killed Vincent Swift. I didn't see how he could have lied so convincingly to Liz. I knew that wasn't a good reason to believe in the man, but I did.

"The Telfers don't have a security system, but their neighbors across the street have a doorbell camera. Mr. Telfer does show up on it, coming home, but it was a lot later than he led you and Liz to believe."

I stared at the floor.

"There may be a perfectly logical explanation for where he went and why he didn't tell you," Mr. P. said.

I looked up at him. "I really want there to be."

"Let me see what I can find."

I rubbed the back of my neck with one hand. "Do I want to know more than that?" I asked.

Mr. P. picked up his coffee. "I think this is one of those times that ignorance is bliss," he said.

Chapter 15

Charlotte and Mac were moving a bookcase when I went back into the shop. I stood and watched as they set it to the right of the nearby rocking chair and then to the left. "It's still not right," Charlotte said after the second move.

Mac folded his arms and stared at the large set of shelves. The bookcase was solid wood and very heavy. And it had been in the store for months. "You're right," he said. "It's not."

I came up beside Charlotte, wrapping my arms around her shoulders. "What are you doing, toots?" I said.

She smiled. "Trying to come up with a way to showcase the bookcase. It's a lovely piece of furniture but everyone ignores it. We're trying to create a cozy reading space but it doesn't look right."

"It looks like we just randomly stuck it in the middle of the room," Mac said.

"Umm, that's kind of what you did," I said. "Can I make a suggestion?"

Charlotte slid her glasses down her nose and looked at me over the top of them. "I don't know. Can you?"

I laughed and kissed her cheek before I dropped my arms. "*May* I make a suggestion?"

"Please do," she said.

"Move those three chairs away from the wall and put the bookcase there. Instead of using books and magazine to dress it, see what we have in that bin in the workroom that's labeled 'Stuff.'"

"I'm not sure I see where you're going," Mac said.

"A lot of people don't buy physical books anymore. They read on tablets and e-readers or their phones. They don't have a collection of books, so they wouldn't look twice at a bookcase."

Charlotte was already nodding her head. "But they might like somewhere to put some family photos or that vase that belonged to their grandmother."

"Exactly."

"I get it," Mac said. "So you want the bookcase where the chairs are. Where do the chairs go?"

I stared at the space for a moment, trying to picture what could be done with the three mismatched chairs. "What if you brought that round table—the small one—in from the workshop and put the chairs around it?"

Charlotte's eyes lit up. "And the teddy bears."

I grinned at her. "Teddy bears' picnic," we both said at the same time.

"Okay, so let's see if I have it all straight. Bookcase there where the chairs are." He pointed at the wall and I nodded.

"Bring in the round table even though we don't have a piece of glass for the top."

"Yes; and for the ninth time, it doesn't need a piece of glass."

"The table and the chairs go where the rocking chair is."

I nodded again.

"So where does the rocking chair go?"

"Over in the corner," I said.

"By the cash desk," Charlotte said.

We smiled at each other.

"So?" Mac said. "Which is it?"

I turned to look at the cash desk. "Charlotte's right," I said. "Over there."

"I like being right," she said. She took the throw off the back of the rocking chair.

"I'll help you with the bookcase," I said to Mac.

He gave me a look of mock outrage. "Are you saying you think I'm not strong enough to move it by myself?" He flexed one arm. "I have muscles, remember?"

"And they're very nice muscles," I said, reaching up to pat his arm.

"I'm more than just a pretty face, you know," he said over his shoulder as he headed out to get the table.

Charlotte and I moved the rocker and the three chairs. Mac came back with the table and he and I set the bookcase by the wall. "Do you need anything else from me?" he asked.

I shook my head. "We're good."

"I need to look at paint. I'll just be in the workshop."

"Flowered tablecloth or the white one?" Charlotte asked. "If we went with the white one we could use that set of red dishes."

I tried to picture the small table with a lacy white cloth and the set of red dishes I'd discovered in the bottom of a mystery box I'd bought for ten dollars at an auction. "I like the idea of using the red dishes. It could be a Valentine's Day teddy bears' picnic."

I went over to the storage area under the stairs and pulled out the three teddy bears that were sitting on one of the shelves. They had been in a bag of fabric I'd gotten for Jess at a flea market.

Charlotte was arranging the chairs around the table. I set the bears on top. "I was talking to Maddie last night," she said. "We're going in on a seed order." Maddie Hamilton was an old friend of both Charlotte and my grandmother. She was an avid gardener and had also been the Angels' very first client.

"How is she?" I asked.

"Happy," Charlotte said. "She's going to be a grandmother."

"That's wonderful news. Maddie will be a fantastic grandmother."

Charlotte stood back, eyed the chairs and then moved the one on the right a little more to the left. "And it turns out she knows—or maybe I should say knew—William Swift. He used to work at Green Gables Nursery. Maddie says he left that job to intern at an organic farm."

"So he's interested in plants and possibly farming."

"It looks that way," Charlotte said. "It seems his father did not consider either job suitable for a Swift."

"That doesn't surprise me," I said. I nudged the bookcase a little more to the left with my hip.

"Maddie is fairly certain that William is somewhere in the northern part of the state." Charlotte was arranging the bears on the chairs. Their heads were barely level with the top of the table "They're all going to have to sit on a little stack of books," she said. "I think I should tell Alfred. It might help him narrow down his search."

I knew she meant to tell him what she'd learned from Maddie, not that the bears needed the equivalent of booster seats.

"Good idea," I said. If William was somewhere in the northern part of the state, that meant he could be four hours or less away from North Harbor. We hadn't had any storms anywhere in the state in over a week. Driving down would have been an easy trip. Maybe he'd made it.

I left Charlotte and the bears and decided to go out to the garage to see if Mac was going to be painting or if I could start sanding the mantel. I found Elvis staring at the back door. "I'm going to talk to Mac. Do you want to come with me?" I asked.

"Mrr," he said.

I bent down and picked him up. We both knew he had no intention of walking.

I had just stepped outside when I saw a woman crossing the parking lot toward me. Her head was down, her collar turned up, and her hands were stuffed in her pockets.

"Mrr," Elvis said, green eyes narrowed in curiosity.

I shrugged. "I don't know."

The woman finally lifted her head and I realized it was Natalie Telfer. "Hi, Sarah," she said, her voice hesitant. "I don't know if you remember me. We ran most of the Back to the Bay race together a couple of years ago."

"I remember you," I said.

She was painfully thin, engulfed by her light brown wool coat as though she had somehow shrunk since she'd bought it. The bones in her wrists seemed to be poking almost through her skin. Her hair was shorter, a tumble of blond, wind-tossed curls and her eyes were sad. Just looking at her made my chest clench in sympathy.

"You were with Liz French when she went to see my husband yesterday morning."

I nodded. "I was."

She noticed Elvis then. "Is this your cat?"

"Merow," he said as though he'd understood the question.

I smiled. "Like he said, yes."

Natalie held out her hand. "He's beautiful." Elvis sniffed with more nosiness than caution and then nuzzled her fingers. "Hello, Elvis," she said, stroking his fur.

He started to purr.

Natalie looked up at me. "I came to ask if you think the police are going to arrest Stella Hall."

"Stella has a lot of friends," I said. "We aren't going to let that happen. She didn't kill Vincent Swift."

Natalie nodded. "I know she didn't. She's a good person." She gave Elvis a small smile. He liked her.

His purr sounded like a car that needed a muffler job. "So is my husband." She exhaled slowly. "I know that he told you he left the library and went home, and that's true, but he didn't go straight home. He went to a bar. He got drunk. But I promise you he didn't kill Mr. Swift."

She was still scratching behind Elvis's ear and he still had the same blissful expression on his face. Given that he always seemed to know when someone was lying, it seemed that Natalie was telling the truth, as far as she knew it.

"I just wanted you to know that," she added. "In case you checked on his story."

"Thank you," I said.

"If, uh . . . if Stella needs anything, if I could help in any way, would you call me, please?"

I nodded. "I will." I didn't know what to do with my hands. I wanted to hug her but I was afraid she would break into a hundred brittle pieces if I did. I swallowed down the lump that was suddenly in the back of my throat. "Natalie, if you need anything, please know that you can call me."

She nodded. "Thank you," she said. She gave Elvis one last scratch. He nuzzled her hand again and then she left, hunched down in her coat against the cold.

I watched her disappear down the sidewalk, then I made my way over to the workshop. "Hey," Mac said, smiling at me. Then the smile faded. "What's wrong?"

I gestured behind me. "Natalie Telfer was just here."

Mac took Elvis from my arms and set him on a

nearby chair. Then he put both hands on my shoulders. "Are you okay?" he asked.

I nodded. "I'm all right. It's just . . . it's painful not to be able to help her."

"What was she doing here?"

"When Liz and I went to see Damian yesterday, he admitted he'd been at the library but he left early and went home. He used a rideshare. He showed me the call log on his phone."

"I take it there's more to the story than that," Mac said. He pressed one hand against my cheek for a moment and then snagged a nearby stool with one foot.

I sat down, one foot on the floor, the other on one of the stool's rungs. "When Mr. P. checked, it turned out Damian only went a few blocks from the library and then he got out. Natalie came to tell me he went to a bar. He got drunk."

"Do you think she was telling the truth?"

"I do," I said. "And so does Elvis."

Mac smiled. "That's good."

I nodded. "It is. I should let Mr. P. know." I looked across the parking lot. "How did I get so lucky?" I asked.

Mac frowned. "What do you mean?"

"The Telfers lost their child. William Swift decided he didn't want to have the same last name as his father because their relationship was so bad. But I got two fathers who loved me, a grandmother with a heart so big she was able to make a new family, and four opinionated, meddling senior citizens who would take on Godzilla if I asked them to."

He smiled. "Godzilla wouldn't stand a chance."

I pulled a hand back through my hair. "I don't spend enough time with Mom and Dad. Gram and John just live upstairs but I can go for a week or more without seeing them. And don't get me started on Liam. He's here for about five minutes and then he's gone again."

Mac grabbed my hand, pulling me to my feet. "As soon as Rose and her crew figure out who killed Vincent Swift, go see your parents for a few days. I can handle things here. Take Isabel to lunch—today, tomorrow, next week. Or take an entire day off and spend it with her. Let the world turn without you for a couple of hours. As for Liam . . ." He looked around the workspace. "I'm pretty sure we still have that big butterfly net out here."

I studied him for a moment. I couldn't imagine my life without him. "How did I get so lucky to get you?" I said.

Mac smiled again and wrapped his arms around me. "I think we both got lucky."

I laid my head against his chest. "I think I'll just stay out here like this all morning."

He kissed the top of my head. "Fine with me," he said, "but you do remember there's no coffee out here, don't you?"

I lifted my head and planted a kiss on his chin. "On the other hand, I should go talk to Mr. P."

Mac laughed. "Good to know you have your priorities straight."

"Are you painting this morning?" I asked.

He shook his head. "No. I need to glue all the joints on that desk you got from Cleveland and do some more work on the drawer."

"So I can start sanding the mantel?"

"Whenever you want to."

"Okay. I need to change my clothes, and I really should let Mr. P. know what Natalie told me."

I turned to go back to the shop and Mac caught my hand, giving it a squeeze before letting go. "Don't worry. You'll figure it all out. You're like the Mighty Morphin Power Rangers."

I looked back over my shoulder, giving him my best *What the heck are you talking about?* look. "The what?" I said.

"The Power Rangers. Together they're invincible. You, Rose, Mr. P., Liz and Charlotte—even Nick. You're Power Rangers." He started to sing, "Go Go Power Rangers! Go Go Power Rangers!"

"You watched way too much TV when you were a kid," I said, shaking my head. The song followed me all the way across the parking lot and somehow Mac's unshakable faith and not-exactly-dead-on superhero analogy made me feel a little better.

Mr. P. was in the staffroom getting a cup of coffee. "Damian Telfer went to a bar," I said without any preamble.

"And got very drunk," he finished.

He was always a step ahead of me. "How did you know?"

"It was just a hunch. I knew where the driver had let Mr. Telfer out. I followed up with several drinking establishments in the area. The bartender in the second one remembered him." He added cream to his mug. "How did you know?" he asked.

I leaned against the counter. "Natalie Telfer was here. I realized that I know her—though not very well. She's a runner. We've done some races together. She remembered me as well."

"So she came to explain where her husband had been."

"Yes. She guessed that we wouldn't just accept his phone log as his alibi." I reached for a clean mug on the shelf. "I'm glad you confirmed exactly where he was."

"I am as well," he said.

"Mac compared us to the Power Rangers," I said. "It's a kids' TV show."

Mr. P. nodded, looking thoughtful. "The analogy is a little loose but I see his point." He picked up his coffee. "I think I'd choose to be the Blue Power Ranger," he said. "Rosie says blue is my color and I would like the double-bladed lance very much." He smiled. "I once took a course in stage fighting. I'm sure it would come back to me." He left, humming to himself. He was halfway down the stairs before I realized it was the Power Rangers theme song. I was starting to get the feeling that Mom had insisted on a little too much fresh air and sunshine on Saturdays. And now the song was stuck in my head.

It was a busy morning. I managed to sand the top and both sides of the mantel. It was slow, tedious work, but in my head I could see how good the piece would look once I was finished and I used that image to keep me inspired. Two minivans of skiers stopped in just before lunch. We sold the record player Mac had repaired along with a stack of old 45s.

"We need a bigger mat here by the door," Charlotte said to me. She was sweeping up the sand the skiers had tracked in.

"I'll put it on my list," I said as I hung up a guitar. I had my fingers crossed that one of the skiers would stop in on the way back and buy it. "We need coffee cream as well."

"And teabags."

"That's Rose's department. She's been keeping us supplied from her stash of Canadian Red Rose."

Rose was convinced the Canadian version of the popular tea was superior to the American. Anytime someone headed across the lines to New Brunswick she would ask them to bring her back a box. She even kept a little cache of Canadian money to make her request as easy as possible.

"I'll remind her," Charlotte said.

I took a step back, realized the guitar was hanging crooked and moved it a little to the right. "Charlotte, do you have any idea who Vincent Swift might have dated before he married his wife?"

"Oh my goodness, that's a long time ago." She stopped sweeping and stared off into space for a moment. "I know he dated Caroline Reeves because they got married. The wedding was quite the event. But before Caroline I don't remember seeing him with anyone or hearing he was seeing someone." She turned to look at me. "Is it important?"

"I don't know," I said. "I'm not really sure what I'm

looking for. It's one of those *I'll know it when I see it* things."

"I'll keep my fingers crossed then," she said.

After lunch I sat at my desk and opened my laptop. Elvis jumped up to help. He sat beside the computer and leaned over to look at the screen. "Your big giant head is in the way," I said. I picked him up and set him on my lap, where he made a few disgruntled murps before he got settled. Since I knew that Vincent Swift had gone to Camden Collegiate, I went to the school's website first, hoping they'd have an archive of old photos from past events at the school. They did. The problem was the archives were only accessible to former students.

"Okay, let's go to plan B," I said to Elvis.

That got an enthusiastic merow.

Plan B was the school's yearbooks. Also only accessible online to former students.

I made a face at the screen and slumped against the back of my chair, one hand stroking the cat's fur. "Do we know anyone who went to Camden Collegiate?" Avery had gone through several schools before she'd settled at her current one but the Camden private school wasn't one of them.

"Mrr," Elvis said.

"Yeah, I didn't think we did," I said. "So where could we find copies of their yearbooks?"

Elvis wrinkled his whiskers like he was trying to think of somewhere.

"Not the library. Remember when we tried to find Gram's graduation picture for her birthday?"

It seemed he didn't. Then it occurred to me that for some people high school yearbooks were historical documents, as full of useful information as a county census list. "The historical society," I said. I straightened up, set Elvis back on the desk and reached for my phone.

The North Harbor Historical Society did have a collection of Camden Collegiate yearbooks and they were happy to let me look through them. (I did a little celebratory fist pump.) They were open until four thirty.

I looked at my watch. The Historical Society office was just a couple of blocks away. I could be there and back in no time. I put on my boots and coat and found my scarf, hat and gloves. Downstairs, Rose and Avery were holding up the ends of a lace-trimmed tablecloth while a young man in red-framed glasses stood in front of it, arms crossed over his chest, frowning. I caught Rose's eyes and pointed at the front door. She nodded. I left before she could ask where I was going.

The North Harbor Historical Society occupied the second floor of a three-story office building, a modern two-tone stone box with windows that didn't open. It took no time for one of the staff members to bring me the yearbooks I wanted. He handed me a pair of cotton gloves to wear and reminded me to be careful as I turned the pages.

Vincent Swift looked ridiculously young and somber in his freshman-class photo. His dark hair was slicked back from his face, his arms stiff at his sides. I found the future Caroline Swift as well. She was tall with lovely posture. Not a strand of her dark hair was out of place.

I moved forward to look at the section of photographs call "Out & About." I didn't see any sign of Vincent. He didn't look any less stone-faced in his class photo for the following year. I started to scan the section of informal pictures. About halfway through, I found what I was looking for: Vincent Swift in a group of young people at what looked like a hockey game. He was smiling. And not a pasted-on smile for the camera. He looked happy. His right arm was around the shoulders of a girl, who was grinning up at him. She wasn't tall. She was tiny. She didn't have sleek, dark hair. She had a tumble of blond curls. I stared at the photo. It couldn't be who I thought it was, could it? I closed my eyes, counted to ten and opened them again. Nothing had changed.

I got to my feet and walked over to the desk. "Excuse me," I said to the young man who had gotten the books for me. "May I take a photo of something in one of those yearbooks?"

"That depends on what it is. You can't take a photo of any of the class pictures. The original photo studio still owns the rights to them."

"This is just an informal shot of some kids standing around at a hockey game. Somebody probably took it on an old Kodak point-and-shoot."

"Let me see," he said. He walked back to the table where I'd been sitting. I pointed at the photograph. "Oh, that's fine. Go ahead." I took two photos of the picture, trying to minimize the glare from the overhead lights. I put my phone away and carried the books back to the desk, peeling off my cotton gloves as well. "Thank you for your help," I said.

He smiled. "You're welcome. I hope you found what you needed."

I thought about saying I didn't need what I'd just found in that yearbook but I just nodded and left.

I walked back to Second Chance trying to tell myself that I was wrong, that the photo was too old and wasn't sharp enough. But I knew I wasn't wrong; the yearbook was in excellent shape and the black-and-white image was clear and detailed.

I went in the back door straight through to the shop. Rose was trying a knitted scarf on one of the bears at the teddy bears' picnic table. She looked up at me and smiled. "You're back. Where did you go?"

I ignored the question. "Avery, I need to borrow Rose," I said.

"Okay," she said, holding out her hand for the scarf Rose had been about to tie around the bear's neck.

Rose's smiled turned into a frown. "What's going on?"

"I need to show you something. You and Mr. P."

"All right. He's in the office. Let's go."

Rose moved fast for a short person. I was right behind her.

Mr. P. looked up from his computer. "Rosie, is everything all right?" he asked

"The person to answer your question is Sarah," she said.

He turned to me, his head tipped to one side. "What's going on?"

"When Mr. Swift's driver, Guy Tremblay, was here, he told us about a conversation they had just a few days before Swift died, about lost loves and roads not taken. Something about it bothered me, I guess. He was talking about the past, and less than a week later the man was dead. You know I'm not crazy about co-incidences."

He nodded.

"Anyway, I ended up at the historical society going through the yearbooks for the time Vincent Swift was in school and I found a photograph." I pulled up on my cell the picture of the kids at the hockey game. I handed the phone to Mr. P. and pointed at the screen. "That's him."

He studied the photo. "It definitely is."

"Look at the girl beside him," I said.

He made that section of the image larger. Rose leaned over his shoulder for a better look.

"Oh my goodness," she said. "That's Stella!"

Chapter 16

I looked at Mr. P. even though I didn't need him to confirm what I'd known since I'd first seen the photo.

"It is Stella," he said. "But you didn't need Rose or me to tell you that."

I scrubbed both hands over my face. "Why didn't she tell us? I thought they hated each other."

"We don't know what this means."

"It means Stella lied."

Rose was already shaking her head. "Stop right there. All Stella told us is that the two of them were on opposite sides of pretty much every issue and because of that they argued a lot. I never heard her say she hated Vincent, and all that photograph tells us is that they were friends when they were kids."

"He has his arm around her."

"Well, if that means that Stella and Vincent were some kind of star-crossed lovers then I guess the same can be said for your grandfather and me because your grandmother has a very similar photo of the two of us."

I just stood there staring at a spot over her right shoulder. "Do you have to be so darn reasonable?" I finally said.

Mr. P. made a sound like he was choking.

Rose patted him on the back. "I think something went down the wrong way," she said. "Do you need a drink?"

He cleared his throat. "I'm fine, Rosie, thank you," he said.

Rose smiled. "Sweet girl, everyone in this room knows I have had the occasional unreasonable moment. I think we should talk to Stella before we make any more assumptions. Can you do that?"

I nodded. "Yes, I can do that."

"All right. I'll call Stella and see how soon she can be here." She took out her phone and moved over by the table.

Mr. P. reached up and patted my hand. "Most of the time we get her fastball, but every once in a while she slips in the curveball."

Stella showed up about forty-five minutes later. We sat at the table in the office.

"Have you found something?" she asked. Elvis had wandered in and was sitting at her feet. She patted her lap and he jumped up. Stella began to stroke his fur. Rose glanced at me. I knew what she was thinking.

"We have found something," Rose said. "I'm not sure how or if it's even connected to the case." Mr. P. had printed a copy of the photo from my phone. She slid it across the table to Stella.

"That's Vincent and me at the boys' state hockey championship game," Stella said.

"He has his arm around you."

She nodded. "It was cold." Then the significance of what Rose has said seemed to sink in.

"No, no, no. We weren't a couple. We were just friends. Good friends, for a while." Stella ran two fingers over the image of herself and Swift. "That was a long time ago."

"What do you mean, 'good friends, for a while'?" Mr. P. asked.

Elvis was purring. So far, it seemed, Stella hadn't said anything that wasn't true.

"We met at a debate tournament and just hit it off. I think because we were the only two people there who liked the process. Everyone else was just in debate because it looked good on a college application. There was nothing romantic between the two of us. And once Vincent's snobby parents found out his debate buddy was a girl from the wrong side of the tracks, that was the end of us spending time together and it was the end of our friendship. I didn't tell you because I didn't think it mattered."

"It doesn't matter," I said.

Elvis tipped his head so Stella could scratch behind his left ear. "This is going to sound crazy, I know, but I wish I had gone back upstairs to talk to him that night."

"Why?' I asked.

"You know how I said he came after me when I walked out of the meeting?"

I nodded.

"It was what he said. I didn't know then it would be the last thing the man ever would say to me."

"What did he say?" Rose asked.

"It's no big deal. He just said, 'Please wait. There's something I want to tell you.' And now I kind of wonder what it was."

Stella left, and I gave Rose a big hug. She smelled like her coconut hand cream. "What's this for?" she asked.

"It's for always having my back."

"I always will, sweet girl," she said. "Always."

The rest of the afternoon went by quickly. Just before four o'clock, a man who had come in and looked at one of our guitars came back for a fourth time, and this time he bought it. "It's a Valentine's Day gift," he said with a shy smile. I tried not to think about the fact that I still didn't have a gift for Mac.

Mac and I went skating at the outdoor rink after supper. My legs were wobbling when we came off the ice. "I guess I'm not in as good shape as I thought," I said.

Mac put his arm around me. "And here I thought I made you weak in the knees."

I smiled at him. "You do."

On Saturday morning, I got up early and went for a run. My legs protested and I was glad to get home and let the hot water of the shower pound on them for a couple of minutes.

Rose came out of her apartment just as I was locking my door. She looked like a little elf in her red hat with the fluffy pompom. Elvis looked up at her, cocking his head to one side. She bent down and picked him up, carrying him out to the SUV. I decided it wasn't worth the effort to give her my "you're spoiling him" speech.

We were headed to the shop, talking about sourdough starter when something suddenly caught Rose's eye. "Pull over, Sarah," she said, reaching out a hand to grab my arm. "Now. Please."

I checked my rearview mirror for traffic and pulled to the curb by a large brick house. "What's wrong?" I said.

She turned in her seat. So did Elvis "The church back there. Did you see the man widening the path to the front doors?"

"Not really." My eyes had been on the road.

"It's Brent," she said.

I stared at her. "Brent LeBlanc. Are you sure?"

"I wouldn't have told you to stop if I wasn't, now would I?"

I'd walked right into that one.

"We have to go talk to him," Rose said.

I knew it was a waste of words to point out that this might not be the best time. I pulled ahead, turned in the next driveway and went back to the church. "You're in charge," I said to Elvis as we got out of the SUV. He moved over onto the driver's seat.

Brent LeBlanc still looked very young. He wore a tan-colored canvas jacket and heavy black gloves. His wavy blond hair was disheveled from shoveling and there was a small scrape and a bruise on his left cheek but his smile was genuine when he recognized Rose.

"I know why you're here, Mrs. Jackson," he said. "I know you're a detective, and I heard about Mr. Swift. You want to know if I killed him, don't you?"

Chapter 17

"Don't be silly," Rose said. "I know you wouldn't do anything like that."

"I really wouldn't," Brent said. "I didn't like the old man but I didn't kill him." He smiled at me. "Hey, Sarah, how are you?"

I smiled back at him. Brent reminded me of a big, friendly golden retriever. "I'm fine," I said.

"Where were you Monday night?" Rose asked.

"I was at the library."

I shot Rose a look. She pretended not to see it.

"Then I was home watching the game."

"What were you doing at the library?" I said.

Brent leaned against his shovel. "Same thing as I'm doing here. I was clearing off the back loading dock." He held up his right arm and I realized it was covered, fingers to elbow with a fiberglass cast. "I was a lot faster then because I didn't have this thing. See, the town crew is supposed to keep that loading dock clear, but they never do and so Ann pays me out of petty cash to shovel snow off the whole thing." He touched the abrasion on his cheek. "That's how I got this. A big chunk of ice came off the roof and I didn't move fast enough. Just about knocked me flat."

Rose smiled and shook her head. "And how did you break your arm?"

"Took a corner too fast, came off my snowmobile and hit a tree. I figure I've still got five or six of my nine lives." He suddenly grinned. "Hold on a second, I wanna show you something." He pulled out his cell, moved through several screens and then turned the phone so we could see it." A tiny blond toddler with Brent's blue eyes was smiling at the camera. "That's Taylor. My daughter."

"She's beautiful," Rose said.

"She is," I agreed.

"Yeah, she mostly looks like her mama." His grin got a little wider. "She talks all the time."

Rose raised an eyebrow. "I wonder where she got that from."

Brent laughed. "I did kinda talk a lot in class, didn't I?" His expression changed. "Taylor's going to have it better than I did. I mean it. I don't want her to ever be ashamed of me, so I'm not going to ever do anything to make her feel that way, which includes killing the old man. I saw him when I was shoveling. But I give you my word I didn't get anywhere near him. I know my word didn't used to mean anything, but it does now."

"I'm glad to hear that," Rose said.

"I got my GED, and I'm going back to school soon. I'm good at fixing things and I'm going to be a plumber. I'm going to give Taylor a good life, Mrs. Jackson."

Rose put one hand on his shoulder. "I am so proud of you."

Brent looked over at me. "Mrs. Jackson was the only person who ever really believed in me."

I smiled. "She's really good at that."

"You know, I saw him leave. Mr. Swift, I mean," Brent said. "There was ice in the parking lot and I was throwing down some sand. I didn't follow him or anything. Ask Ann. She was by the side door. She could see me."

"Did you see anyone else who you know had problems with Mr. Swift?" I asked.

Brent gave a snort of laughter. "That would be a lot of people."

I noticed how his eyes flicked away from my face. "Were any of them there at the library?"

Brent hesitated, shifting a bit uncomfortably from one foot to the other. "I don't want to get anyone in trouble."

"You won't," Rose said.

"I saw Earle Weyman but Earle didn't see me. And Earle wouldn't kill the old man."

"We know about Earle," I said.

"And there was the woman who followed Mr. Swift but I don't know who that was."

"Wait a minute," I said. "You saw a woman follow Mr. Swift?" I looked at Rose again. This time she didn't pretend not to see me.

"Well, I'm not sure she was following him," Brent said. "She might have just been going the same way. I'm not even a hundred percent sure it was a woman."

"What did this person look like?" Rose asked.

He shrugged. "I don't know. I was too far away. Do you think it was the person who killed Mr. Swift?"

"No," I said firmly. "I don't."

When we got to Second Chance, Mr. P. was starting across the parking lot. Rose told him about seeing Brent shoveling at the church. "I'll call Ann a little later," Rose said, "but I tend to believe what Brent told us. He was never a liar."

"Do you think the woman he saw was Stella?" Mr. P. asked.

"She seems the most likely person. And the timing is right."

I unlocked the back door and set Elvis on the floor. "I'll call Cleveland if he doesn't show up today." I smiled at Mr. P. "I don't suppose you happened to stumble over any suspects on your way here, did you?"

He shook his head. "Sadly, I did not." Then he smiled. "But I have found William. He owns an organic farm up in Presque Isle."

I held up one hand and we high-fived. "Road trip," I asked.

He nudged his glasses up his nose. "It seems very likely."

Avery stepped in the back door then. "Hey, guys," she said.

"Aren't you supposed to be in school?" Rose asked. She reached over and brushed snow off the arm of Avery's jacket.

"Yeah, there was a flood at my school so everything's closed for the day." She looked at me. "Do you need me?"

"I thought you had online classes if the school was closed?" I said.

She nodded and picked at a loose thread on her scarf. "We're supposed to, but the thing is, the teachers have to be able to teach those from the school and no one is allowed in the building so there aren't even online classes."

She didn't seem very broken up about it. One of us could have called the school to check but I doubted that Avery would go to so much trouble to avoid her classes. She was smart enough to know Liz would find out.

"You can work on the mantel Mac bought."

Avery smiled. "Cool. And I have some window stuff to do." She looked at Rose. "I'll make the tea, and we all know Mac already made the coffee."

Rose smiled back at her. "Thank you, dear."

"Tea or coffee, Mr. P.?" Avery asked.

"Tea, please," he said.

Avery glanced at me. "I'll get you coffee if Mac didn't already do it." She headed for the shop, stopping to scoop up Elvis without missing a step.

Rose and I were in the Angels' office looking over Mr. P.'s shoulder at the website for Dream Catcher Farms, William (Swift) Reeves's farm, when Avery brought down the tea and my coffee.

She glanced at the screen. Mr. P. had brought up a photo of William standing by what looked to be a chicken coop. "The dude looks better there than with the beard and long hair he has now."

I turned to look at her. "What do you mean?"

Avery gestured at the laptop. "The guy right there.

He doesn't look like that anymore. Now his hair's long and kinda scruffy and he has a beard. It's sorta mangy, too."

"How do you know what he looks like now?" Mr. P. asked.

"Duh," she said. "'Cause I saw him."

"Saw him where?" I said.

"At the farmers' market."

"Was this recently, Avery?" Mr. P. asked

She nodded. "Yeah. Last night." She pointed at the computer screen. "And that guy right there was at one of the stalls. It looked like he was working there."

"Do you remember which stall?" Rose said.

"Sure. It was the sprout guy. That's actually what he calls his business, which isn't very creative if you ask me."

I gave her a look.

She almost rolled her eyes but stopped herself. "Fine. I'm just saying. Anyway, I've never seen him there before but he was definitely helping sprout guy and they acted like they were friends."

"Where is sprout guy's stall?" I said.

"About half way down on the left-hand side. He has more than sprouts, you know." This time she gave me a look. "If you wanted to, say, make a smoothie for breakfast, he has baby spinach and little tiny beets."

From the corner of my eyes I could see that Rose was trying to stifle a smile. "That's sounds very healthy," she said. She was looking right at me.

"Maybe I'll get some beets and spinach and make a smoothie one morning for breakfast . . . for Rose and me," I said. "Thanks for telling me."

Rose made a strangled sound beside me and started to cough.

Avery reached over and patted her back. "You also need a banana, some berries, an apple and whatever plant milk you like best. And buy organic stuff."

I nodded.

"I'll email you the recipe."

"Thank you," I said.

"Do you guys want anything else?" she asked.

Mr. P. shook his head. "Thank you for making the tea and bringing it down. And Sarah's coffee as well."

She smiled. "No problem. I have to go see if Mac needs me to do anything before I start on the mantel."

Once she was gone I handed Rose her tea. "I'm sure it will help your dry throat."

"She's going to ask you if you tried that drink every day until you do," she said.

I picked up my coffee and took a long, satisfying drink. There was no way any drink with beets and spinach was going to taste so good. "Who's to say I'm not going to try it?"

Rose pulled herself up to her full not quite five feet. "Making healthy changes is always a good idea." She had a little edge of self-righteousness in her tone.

I folded my arms over my chest. "A green smoothie sounds like a good way to start the day." I sounded even more sanctimonious than Rose had.

Mr. P. cleared his throat. "With beets, I think the color would be a little closer to pink."

Rose and I exchanged a look. I'm not sure which one of us started to laugh first.

"What have you gotten us into?" she said.

"Me?" I said. "You're the one who said it sounded 'very healthy.'" I made air quotes around very healthy.

"I said that, didn't I? I was trying to be positive."

"Now I'm going to have to swallow some pink drink with flecks of spinach floating around in it." I shuddered.

"We could use my blender. It can pulverize an ice cube right back to water."

Mr. P. cleared his throat again. We both turned to look at him. He tapped the computer screen with one finger. "William Swift, aka William Reeves," he said.

"Sorry," I said. Rose and I had driven the conversation into a ditch, up the other side and onto a whole new road.

"He is Vincent Swift's next of kin. It makes sense that he would be in town. That should have occurred to me. I'm afraid I've had tunnel vision."

Rose patted his arm. "It seems we all did, Alfred," she said.

"Do you two want to go to the market after supper?" I asked.

Mr. P. nodded. "I think we should." He gave us a sly smile. "After all, you two have some shopping to do."

Cleveland showed up just before eleven. For a while his cousin had worked with him, but I hadn't seen the man in months. Cleveland had an armoire standing upright in the back of his old pickup, lashed to one side of the truck bed with bungee cords. The doors of the armoire were covered with gold-veined mirror tiles. Mac's eyes lit up at the sight of the heavy piece of furniture. As fast as we worked on one and stuck it in the shop we'd have a sale. We had even sold one armoire as we were moving it across the parking lot from the old garage.

"Real wood?" Mac said to Cleveland.

He nodded. "Hang on and you can take a look inside." He reached around the side of the armoire and unfastened two of the bungee cords. He was a strong, solid man, ex–army intelligence. I'd never heard him talk about his service, but if there were a project anywhere in the area benefiting veterans, Cleveland would be there. That's how we'd first met.

Mac climbed up and opened one of the mirrored doors. "Is this cedar inside?"

"It's pretty much lost its smell but if you give it a light sanding that should bring it back."

"What are you asking?" I said to Cleveland. He named a number that was a little higher than I had expected but wasn't unreasonable, either.

I looked in the truck bed to see what else he had. A distressed desk painted a vivid shade of robin's-egg blue was on its side behind the armoire. "Tell me about the desk."

"I think the color is a bit too much for most people, and the drawer is broken," Cleveland said. "It's missing the bottom and half of one side."

"What do you want for it?"

He named an amount that was less than I'd thought he'd say. Mac was checking the legs and running a hand over the blue painted sides. "We could do something with this," he said.

I poked around in a large cardboard box that was

filled with books and maps. I found three of the later that I liked.

Cleveland gave me the total and I paid him in cash. No negotiating. Then he climbed into the back of the truck to help Mac lift out the armoire.

"Any chance you'd have a needle for an old record player?" Mac asked.

"I think so," Cleveland said. "Show me the record player."

They set the armoire inside the workshop and Mac lifted the turntable down from a nearby shelf. He'd spent days carefully removing layers of grime from it.

"I have one or two needles that should work," Cleveland said. "I'll bring them by tomorrow."

"Do you have a second?" I said after he and Mac had taken the desk into the old garage space.

"Sure. What's up?"

"I need to ask you about Earle Weyman."

He nodded. "I figured someone would when I heard about Vincent Swift."

I stuffed my hands in my coat pockets. I'd left my gloves inside. "I don't think Earle killed the man, but someone put him at the library that night. Stella is the Angels' client and my friend. Maybe Earle saw something. I know it's a long shot."

"You busy right now?" he asked.

I shook my head. "No."

"Earle is doing some painting at the house Memphis bought. We can go right now and talk to him."

I didn't even stop to think about it. "Yes," I said.

"We'll take my truck and I'll bring you back."

I told Mac where I was going. "Cross your fingers."

"I'll hold down the fort," he said. "Good luck."

"When did Memphis buy a house?" I asked Cleveland as he turned out of the parking lot.

"The week before Christmas. You know Clayton McNamara?"

I nodded. "I do." I reached one hand toward the nearest heat vent. The truck may have been old but the heater worked well.

"It's just down the road from his place."

Clayton McNamara lived at the far end of North Harbor, close to the water. It was a beautiful spot.

"The house was a rental and the tenants trashed the place. Owner lives out of state and I guess he'd just had enough. He was looking for a quick sale so Memphis got a good deal. There's a big chunk of property and a huge garage that was in a lot better shape than the house."

"Good for Memphis," I said. "If he needs anything, tell him to come into the shop. I'll give him the friends and family discount."

Cleveland stopped to let a car turn left into a driveway. He glanced over at me. "If you've got a decent kettle I'll buy it from you. I'm getting sick of boiling water for coffee in an old pot on the even older stove in his kitchen."

I smiled. "I'll see what I can find for you."

The house Memphis had bought was a small saltbox, two floors in the front and one in the back with the distinctive long sloped roof and unadorned front. The white paint on the outside was crinkling and peeling everywhere.

"New clapboards are a project for the spring,"

Cleveland said as we got out of the truck. He pointed at the roof. "That came first."

The driveway continued past the little house, ending at a large outbuilding that did look, at least on the outside, to be in better shape than the house.

"That's the garage," Cleveland said. "I figure maybe I can convince Memphis to let me use it for storage down the road."

Inside the house was clean and bright, flooded with sunshine from the big multi-pane windows.

Earle was in the living room in jeans and a long-sleeved, paint-spattered T-shirt painting the ceiling. "Hey, Cleveland," he said. Then he caught sight of me. "Sarah Grayson. What are you doing out here?"

I didn't see any point in dancing around my reasons for being there. "I came to ask you about Vincent Swift."

His expression darkened. "If you think I'm going to say I'm sorry he's dead, I'm not."

"He wasn't a very nice person," I said.

Earle didn't say anything. This was not starting out well. On the other hand, I had kind of ambushed the man.

"You know Alfred Peterson is a private investigator," Cleveland said.

Earle nodded. "Yeah, I know."

"You probably heard that Memphis and I sometimes do a bit of security stuff for him."

Earle shrugged. I took that as a yes.

The laces of Cleveland's left boot were untied. He bent down to fasten them. Earle shifted uncomfortably from one foot to the other.

Had this been a mistake, I wondered? Maybe Mr. P. should have come with me. Or come instead of me.

"Look," Cleveland said. "Alfred's office is in Sarah's building. Sometimes she helps out. She isn't going to blab all over town about your business. Just talk to her."

"What do you want to know?" Earle said. He didn't quite meet my gaze.

"Stella Hall found Swift lying in the street," I said.

"Sorry to hear that. Stella is a good woman."

I nodded. "Yes, she is, and I don't want Stella to get blamed for something you and I know she wouldn't have done."

"So you think I did something to him?" Earle said. Even with the distance between us I could see his jaw tighten.

Beside me, Cleveland gave a sigh of exasperation. "C'mon, Earle. Hang on and hear her out."

Earle was angry and defensive. Considering what he'd gone through, it made sense. I probably would have reacted the same way if it had been me. "I don't think you did anything to Mr. Swift," I said, "but someone saw you at the library that night. I just want to know if you saw Swift and if you did, was there anyone with him?"

"I saw him," Earle said. "He looked right through me as though he didn't know who I was. I don't think he did. The guy was an ass. I'm not surprised someone killed him. Wasn't me."

"If I thought it was you, do you think I'd be standing here right now? I would have just called the police." I could hear the frustration in my voice. I took a deep breath and let it out slowly. "The car accident and the lawsuit messed up a lot of lives. I don't want the same thing to happen to Stella because she was in the wrong place at the wrong time."

Earle stared up at the ceiling for a moment. Then he looked at me again. "The girl who was killed in the accident, her father was there. No one would blame that man if he killed Swift. He put the whole thing in motion when he let that boy drive that night."

"Mr. Telfer has an alibi," I said.

"Good."

There was something in his body language, something in the way he wouldn't quite look me in the eye that made me think there was something he wasn't saying. "Earle, what were you doing at the library?" I asked.

"Oh for heaven's sake, tell her," Cleveland said.

"I don't want my business spread all over town."

"Your business is your business," I said. "You say you didn't kill Vincent Swift and I believe you, but I've also been burned by taking someone at their word so it would help if you'd tell me what the heck you were doing!" I'd gotten a little louder than I'd meant to but I was all out of patience. Mr. P. was much better at this than I was.

Earle squared his shoulders. "I'm learning to read. I never really got the hang of it in school. I want a job with opportunities and so I go to the library for tutoring. You know Caroline Vega? She paints." He gestured at the tray on the floor. "Not this kind of paint. She's an artist. She's my tutor."

"I know Caroline," I said. We'd met on one of the Angels' cases.

"Call her," Earle said. "She'll tell you. I wouldn't have killed old man Swift. Not when things are finally starting to go my way."

"You should be proud of yourself, Earle," I said.

For the first time since I'd told him why I was there, he looked straight at me and he smiled. "I am," he said.

Chapter 18

Cleveland drove me back to the shop. I thanked him and he said he'd be back tomorrow with the record player needle he'd promised Mac.

Rose and Mr. P. were in the office. "What did you find out?" Rose asked.

"Earle has an alibi," I said. "I can't tell you what it is because it's something personal, but it isn't Earle." I was going to call Caroline Vega, but I was sure she'd confirm Earle's story.

"That's fine," Mr. P. said.

Rose smiled. "Come have chicken potpie with Alfred and me and then we can go to the market."

Mac poked his head around the office door. "I have a paint question when you have a minute," he said to me.

"How do you feel about chicken potpie?" Rose asked him.

"I have very good feelings about it." He looked slightly confused.

"Then come for supper tonight. Afterward we're going to the market to look for Vincent Swift's son."

Mac smiled. "That sounds like a delicious and productive evening. I'd love to come."

Rose clasped her hands together. "Splendid."

I pointed at the ceiling. "I'm going to put my things in my office."

"How did it go?" Mac asked as walked through the workroom.

"It's not Earle," I said. "And I can't say I'm unhappy about that."

"Vincent Swift didn't seem to have a shortage of people who didn't like him. I have faith in Rose and Alfred." He smiled. "And you."

"What was your paint question?" I asked.

"Avery got all the tape off the top of the mantel. I can start her sanding. Are you going to want to use paint or stain? I'm thinking paint."

I nodded. "So am I. Stain will require a lot more sanding and we won't be able to charge much more."

"I agree," he said. Mac looked at his watch. "Lunch in maybe forty-five minutes?"

"Sounds good," I said.

I went up to my office. Mac went back out to the garage.

I hung up my coat, put on my shoes and got a cup of coffee. Then I tried Caroline Vega. I caught her at home and explained why I was calling.

"It's good to hear from you, Sarah," she said. "I am tutoring Earle. He's a very committed student. We were working at the library Monday night. I can tell you that the ambulance went by just as we were leaving. Does that help you?"

Caroline had been on the edges of a murder investigation before. She had to know why I was asking about Earle.

"It does," I said. "Thank you."

We agreed we'd try to go running together soon and said good-bye.

Mac and I had lunch out in the old garage. I sent Avery inside to eat. "There's a bowl on the counter with a cloth napkin on top," I said. "I saved the last two oatmeal chocolate chip cookies for you."

"Thanks, Sarah," she said with a grin.

Mac and I spent most of our lunch break deciding what to do with the armoire. The mirrored tiles seemed like they'd been cemented into place and I wasn't sure how we were going to get them off. "I guess we could break them if we have to?"

Mac's mouth twisted to one side. "I'm not really comfortable with doing that."

"I didn't know you were superstitious," I said, tipping my head sideways, trying to peer under the edge of one of the outer tiles to see what exactly had been used to fasten them to the door. "Aside from your hockey stuff."

"I'm not superstitious," he said, "but Elvis is out here all the time. It's way too easy to end up with tiny glass slivers on the floor if we break any of those tiles. As it is, I'm going to put down a tarp to work on. And what do you mean, 'aside from your hockey stuff'?"

"I mean that whole *You won't wash your jersey during the playoffs* thing."

"That's not superstition, it's tradition. It's ritual. That's completely different."

"Of course it is," I said, shaking my head instead of nodding.

It was maybe an hour later when Neill Halloran and his assistant, Henry Davis, came into the shop. "Judge Halloran, It's so good to see you," I said. Although he was no longer on the bench most people still called Neill Halloran "Judge," an indication of how well-respected he was. The judge looked far less imposing than his reputation suggested. He was a little under six feet and a bit stoop-shouldered, with thinning hair, sharp blue eyes behind wire-framed glasses and two discreet hearing aids. He wore a black woolen coat and a plaid scarf at his neck.

"Hello, Sarah," he said with a warm smile. "It's good to see you as well." He took one of my hands in both of his. "Goodness, your hands are cold."

I smiled at him. "You know what Gram would say."

He nodded. "Cold hands, warm heart. How is Isabel?"

"She's well. I'll tell her you asked about her." I turned to Henry. "It's good to see you, too, Henry."

"And you, Sarah," he said. Henry Davis was five foot nine, give or take an inch. He had dark eyes and dark skin. His scalp was shaved smooth and he had a closely cropped salt-and-pepper beard and mustache. He wore a camel-colored jacket with a green scarf knotted at his neck.

"What are you two doing here?" I asked.

"I heard the Angels have taken Stella Hall on as a

client and I expected to hear from them. When I didn't, I decided to take the bull by the horns." He gave my hands one last gentle squeeze and let them go.

I frowned. "Why did you expect to hear from them?"

"They must be looking at possible suspects and I should be on that list," he said, his voice matter-of-fact. "I never cared for the man and we had been on opposite sides of the very contentious debate over what to do with the money that had been left to the library. For the record, I agree with Stella."

"You don't belong on any suspect list," I said. "You couldn't kill anyone."

He gave me that lovely warm smile again. "I appreciate your belief in me, but you're letting your personal feelings affect your judgment. You're like your grandmother."

Gram and Judge Halloran had been friends in high school and had even gone out a couple of times. He still had a soft spot for her.

I smiled back at him. "Thank you for the compliment."

"The judge has an alibi for the time of Mr. Swift's murder," Henry said just as Rose came down the stairs.

"Hello, Neill," she said. "You're looking well."

"As are you, Rose," he said.

She turned to Henry. "You said Neill has an alibi?"

He nodded. "He was with me. I picked him up from the library after Mr. Swift left."

"He did," the judge said. "I'm not so far gone that I don't remember that."

"If you have a few minutes, I'd like to hear more about the battle between Vincent Swift and Stella," Rose said.

"I'd be happy to tell you what I know."

Rose smiled. "Excellent. Come back to the office."

"How about a cup of tea?" I asked.

"Thank you, my dear, I'd like that," he said.

Avery had been arranging a collection of tiny vases on the bookshelf Mac had moved. "I'll get it, Sarah," she said. She headed for the stairs.

"If it's not too much trouble, I'm wondering if you could show me a guitar?" Henry said. "My nephew has been talking about wanting to learn to play." He looked at Judge Halloran. "You don't mind, do you?"

He shook his head. "Of course not, but your sister might."

Henry nodded. "I'll keep that in mind."

Rose and the judge headed for the Angels' office and Henry walked over to the collection of instruments we had hanging on the back wall.

I joined him. "You don't really want to look at guitars, do you?

He smiled. "No. My nephew already plays the drums. The judge is right: If I showed up with a guitar my sister would shoot me."

"Is there something you didn't want to say in front of Judge Halloran?"

He looked past me for a moment then his gaze came back to my face. "Yes, there is. I have more of a motive to want Mr. Swift dead."

I stared at him, dumbfounded. "You?" I said. "I don't understand."

"As he said, the judge was siding with Ms. Hall about how to spend the bequest to the library. But Mr. Swift had been using the judge's Alzheimer's diagnosis to devalue his credibility. Yes, he forgets things sometimes but there's nothing wrong with his critical reasoning skills. I wrote a letter to every member of the board telling them that."

"And that didn't go over well with Mr. Swift."

Henry shook his head. "Mr. Swift felt my letter denigrated his abilities. He threatened to sue me for libel."

I sighed. "I wish I could say that surprises me."

"Then, out of the blue, a very well-respected civil lawyer from Portland contacted me. He'd been paid a retainer by someone who wanted to remain anonymous. He felt there was no case. I hadn't said anything that wasn't true and couldn't be proved. He contacted Mr. Swift's lawyer and the whole thing disappeared."

"I'm glad," I said. I wondered if the anonymous person had been Liz. It was the kind of thing she'd do. "And don't forget: You're Judge Halloran's alibi, which makes him yours."

Henry shook his head. "His memory isn't always good. He can remember something he did when he was twelve but he doesn't always know what he had for breakfast."

I tipped my head to one side and studied him for a moment. "Did you kill Vincent Swift?"

"Of course not. I wished more than once that the man would disappear but I didn't kill him." One hand played with the scarf at his neck. "There's something else I need to tell you. When I went to get the car I saw Mr. Swift leave, and just a couple of minutes later I saw a woman follow him." He took a deep breath and let it out slowly. "Sarah, I think it could have been Ms. Hall. Whoever it was had the same light-colored hair and they were wearing a tan-colored coat with the collar turned up. She was wearing a jacket like that. I saw her in it before the meeting started."

My stomach flip-flopped. "It could have been anyone," I said. "Except for the hair and gender, you could have just described yourself."

"The woman came from the library just minutes after Mr. Swift left," Henry said. "She looked up and down the street then headed in the direction he had gone. She was walking with a purpose."

"Have you told this to the police?" I asked.

He shook his head. "I'm not certain who I saw. It looked like Stella Hall but I didn't have my glasses on. They had steamed up when I got in the car and, as well, the streetlight in front of the library is burned out."

"So you saw somebody who may or may not have been Stella, who may or may not have even been a woman and may or may not have followed Vincent Swift."

"It doesn't sound so definitive when you put it that way," Henry said.

"I don't think there's anything to worry about," I said. I wished my stomach believed that.

Henry looked at the guitar closest to him. "That's a beautiful instrument," he said.

I nudged his shoulder. "You're not too old to learn to play."

"But I am too tone-deaf."

I showed Henry a couple of guitars. "I think I'll float the idea with my sister," he said. "A guitar would make less noise than drums."

"Not necessarily," I said. "But you don't have to tell her that part."

Rose and Judge Halloran came back. "Thank you for answering our questions," she said.

He smiled. "Thank you for actually being interested in my answers." He turned to me. "Sarah, please thank your grandmother for . . ." He frowned. "I can't remember. It was right on the tip of my tongue and now it's gone."

"The cookies," Henry said quietly.

The judge's face cleared. He nodded. "That's right. They were oatmeal with raisins and they were very good."

I nodded. "I'll tell her."

After they left, Rose turned to me. "What did Mr. Davis want to talk to you about?"

"You knew," I said.

"I may have been born at night but it wasn't last night."

I rubbed the back of my neck with one hand. "He thought he might have seen Stella follow Swift when he left the library. Henry didn't have his glasses on and it was dark. I don't see how he could be right. He described her coat accurately but that's it. It can't have been Stella. She hired us."

"We need the security footage from the camera at

the front of the library," Rose said. "Ann has been stalling on it but I'll get after her." She patted my arm. "Don't fret. There's a logical explanation for this. Stella Hall did not kill anyone."

"You're right," I said. But a tiny voice inside my head whispered, *But who did?*

Chapter 19

I drove Rose home and Mr. P. decided to ride with Mac. When I picked Elvis up he squirmed and wiggled in my arms until I set him down again. Then he walked purposefully across the parking lot, sat down next to the driver's door of Mac's truck and meowed loudly. Mac looked at me, grinned and unlocked the door. Elvis jumped up onto the seat.

"What is this?" I asked.

"We're having a dude hang," Mr. P. said.

I was pretty sure I hadn't heard him correctly. "Excuse me?"

Mac rested on hand on the roof of the truck. "We're having a dude hang. Just guys."

"No chicks," Mr. P. added helpfully.

I rubbed the space between my eyes and walked over to my SUV without saying another word.

"Isn't Elvis coming with us?" Rose asked as she climbed in.

"No, he is not," I said. I fastened my seatbelt and

started the car. "He's with Mac and Mr. P. Apparently the three of them are having a dude hang."

"That's lovely," Rose said. "Since it's just us, you can tell me what you've decided to do for Valentine's Day. A few days ago when we talked about it, you didn't have any plans."

A few days ago when we'd talked about Valentine's Day, Rose had hinted that she and Mr. P. had matching tattoos. I was still trying to get that image out of my mind.

"I have a couple of ideas," I hedged.

"Have you decided to go out or stay in?" I could feel her eyes on me. I kept my own gaze fixed on the road in front of me.

"Maybe we'll stay in."

"Staying in can be very romantic," Rose said. "You could make my flourless chocolate cake. Mac likes that. The good thing about that recipe is you can make it several days in advance. What are you thinking about for a main course?"

"I have no plans," I blurted. I didn't look at her.

"I know you haven't made any final decisions, but as I said, I'll help you with the cake. It's not hard to make."

"I have no plans at all. Not even maybe, kinda, what-if plans. I don't have a present. I don't have an idea for a present. I don't even have any red construction paper so I can make a card. I have nothing."

"I have twinkle lights," Rose said. "You could borrow them." She reached over and patted my arm. "It's not the end of the world if you don't know exactly what you want to do."

"Nothing feels right," I said. "Every suggestion you made is good, but none of them feel like Mac. This is our first Valentine's Day and I want the gift to be perfect."

I glanced over at her. She smiled. "I understand, but the gift doesn't have to be perfect. It just has to come from you."

We pulled into the driveway at home, and Mac parked at the curb. "I need to have a shower and then we'll be right there for supper," I said to Rose.

"That's fine, dear," she said.

I unlocked the apartment door, kicked off my boots and hung up my jacket. "You know, this room had all black walls the first time I saw it," I said to Mac. "And a red ceiling."

He shook his head. "The only thing I can think of is: Why?"

"I don't know. You could ask Liam; he might know. The woman who was living here when I came to see the house had painted the entire apartment."

Mac was looking up at the ceiling, trying perhaps to imagine it painted blood red. "Without the owner's permission, I'm guessing."

"You'd think. But no. Anyway, Liam went out with her at least twice so he may know the reason behind the color scheme."

"I'm still impressed with how you managed to trade your way into a down payment."

I grinned. "Yeah, it was one of my more creative moments. I was cleaning out that barn to make a little money. I had no idea there was an entire Volkswagen in there. Or that the woman would let me have it just to get rid of it." I shook my head. "I had no idea there was a dead raccoon in the car, either."

Mac laughed.

"It's not funny. It was sitting in the driver's seat and it was basically mummified. Jess was convinced we could make a little extra money by selling it to the biology department."

"Did you?" he asked.

"No," I said. I ducked my head. "They didn't want it."

Mac started laughing again.

"Are you laughing at my resourcefulness?" I asked, trying and failing to look indignant.

He shook his head. "No. I'm laughing at the mental image of you and Jess carrying a mummified raccoon to the biology department."

"Just so you know, we didn't carry it. We pushed it in a grocery cart."

Mac held up one hand. He was still shaking with laughter. "So the Bug got traded for a camper van."

"No. I got an old MG for the Bug. I got the camper van for the MG and I lived in that for six months. Then I traded it for the cabin. Jess and I lived there for our last year of college. Then I used the cabin as the down payment on this house, and here we are."

He leaned over and kissed me. "You really were very resourceful," he said.

"Merow," Elvis said as though he'd been listening and agreed with Mac.

"Thank you," I said. I gestured in the general direction of the couch. "Talk among yourselves. I'm taking a shower."

I had a very quick shower and managed for the most part to keep my hair dry. I pulled on my favorite pair of jeans and a blue sweater and went back to the living room to find Mac emptying the dishwasher and Elvis sitting on a stool watching and seemingly listening to Mac talk about the playoff chances of the Minnesota Wild.

"How did you become such a Wild fan?" I asked. "You live on the East Coast. You should be cheering for the Bruins."

Mac smiled as he put two plates in the cupboard. "I saw Crazy Eddie Sweeney play years ago and that did it. Man, could he skate."

"Merow," Elvis said with enthusiasm.

"See?" Mac said. "Elvis gets it."

I smelled the chicken potpies baking when we stepped out into the hallway.

"I'm starting to suspect you may have had an ulterior motive for inviting Rose to move in here," he said. "Assuming she cooks like this all the time."

I tapped on the apartment door and smiled at him. "No comment; and yes, she does."

Mr. P. let us in. He was wearing a Mondrian print apron and the table was set with a dark blue cloth, blue-and-green-plaid napkins and two tall tapers in glass candleholders.

"This is beautiful," I said. "You didn't have to go to all this trouble for us."

Mr. P. smiled. "It's Friday. We do things a little more special on Friday."

"Are we intruding on date night?" Mac asked.

Rose was bent over, peering through the oven door window. "You're not intruding on anything," she said.

The potpie was delicious and we also had a small salad with lettuce, sprouts and radish.

Mac and I cleaned up while Rose objected it wasn't necessary.

"You're not paying the slightest bit of attention to what I'm saying," she said, standing in the middle of the floor with her hands on her hips, looking a lot like a gnome minus the big hat.

"No, I am not," I said as I put the knives and forks in the dishwasher. "I can't imagine where I learned such appalling behavior."

I drove us all to the farmers' market in my SUV, managing to squeeze into a very tight parking spot on the street close to the main doors.

Rose looked over her shoulder. "Are you going to be able to pull out when it's time to leave?" she asked.

"Have I ever not gotten out of a parking spot?" I said.

"There's a first time for everything."

My driving—and parking—made her a little nervous. Riding with Liz was even worse, and I couldn't remember the last time Rose had gotten in a vehicle with Nick.

The market was busy but not overly crowded. There was plenty of space in the aisles and lots of light. And so much enticing looking food: cheese, jam, round, fat loves of sourdough, sauerkraut, yogurt, organic meat and bunches of herbs hanging from wooden drying racks. Everywhere I turned there was something else to look at, something else I wanted to try.

"The market has been open since Thanksgiving; why haven't I come here sooner?" I said. I was mostly thinking out loud but Mr. P. tipped his head to one side and looked inquiringly at me.

"Why haven't you?" he asked.

"I don't have a good reason." And I felt a little embarrassed. "Is this your first visit?"

He shook his head. "Oh no. I've been here several times with Avery."

Avery had a contentious relationship with her parents. That was why she'd come to live with Liz. She spent a lot of time with Rose and Mr. P., which was good for her.

Mac spotted the booth we were looking for just where Avery had said it would be, on the left side of the market space. "I don't see anyone who looks like the photo you showed me," he said.

Neither did I. I didn't see a sign that said SPROUT GUY, either. "Crap," I muttered.

Then a man who had been bent over a large wooden crate stood up.

"That's William," Mr. P. said.

It was. As Avery had said, his hair was longer than in the photo on his website and he had a somewhat unkempt beard, but it was William Swift, aka William Reeves standing in the booth.

"So what do we do?" I said.

Rose frowned. "We go over there and talk to him, of course."

We walked around to the booth and Mr. P. offered William his card. William studied it for a moment. "You have questions about my father," he said.

Mr. P. nodded. "Yes, we do."

William pointed to a small area with a collection of brightly painted tables and chairs. "Why don't we go have a seat?"

"I'm going to take a look around," Mac said in a low voice. "I'll be back."

I followed Mr. P. and Rose to the seating area. The tables and mismatched chairs were all painted in bright primary colors. We sat at a deep blue table with two red chairs and two yellow chairs.

Up close, I could see how much William looked like his father. They had the same chin and the same piercing deep-set eyes.

"We're sorry for your loss," Mr. P. said.

William rested his forearms on the table and laced his fingers together. "Thank you," he said. "You probably know my father was more likely to antagonize people than to make close connections. And that included me."

"May I ask why you changed your name?" Mr. P. asked.

William looked down at his hands. "My father wanted a lawyer or a businessman for a son. Not a farmer. After my mother died, we spent less and less time with each other. It was easier for both of us. Then a couple of years ago, I moved north."

He looked up. "This time last year I came back to see my father. The farm I'd been working at was for sale. I wanted to buy it. I asked my father to loan me the money; I wasn't looking for a handout. I was prepared to pay the going rate of interest. I even put together a five-year business plan."

"He turned you down," Rose said.

"He said farming was a waste of time." He gestured to the people all around us. "Does this look like a waste of time? He told me I was a disappointment. I told him he was a lousy father."

"I'm sorry to hear that," Mr. P. said.

I thought about my own dad, who technically was my stepfather—not that it mattered to either of us. He'd always been my biggest cheerleader, a couple of times even with pompoms.

William shifted in his seat. "Mr. Peterson, I loved my father but I didn't like him. When I got back to Presque Isle, I started the process to change my name. Reeves was my mother's name. It keeps me connected to at least part of my family."

"And you bought the farm," I said.

William looked at me and smiled. "Yes, I did. My friends all chipped in to help me make the down payment on the farm and that was a lot better than being in debt to my father. At this point, I don't know if I've been cut out of his will or not. If I inherit anything from his estate I'll use it to pay back my friends, then the bank, and I'll give away the rest. I'm just here long enough to organize a service for my father and then I'm going home. For the record, I was at the farm on Monday night taking part in an online talk about sustainable farming practices. Please feel free to check."

He studied his hands for a moment and then looked at each of us in turn. "My father wanted to see me. The Thursday before he died he called me. It was the first time that he'd reached out in the last year. I've seen his lawyer on three occasions in the last twelve months—each time she delivered some jewelry that belonged to my mother. The lawyer said that Dad was going through the contents of his safe-deposit box, but I wondered if maybe it was a way to check up on me."

William shrugged. "Anyway, I didn't actually speak to my father when he called. He left a message. He said he'd heard some news he wanted to talk to me about. He asked me to come for a visit. My"—he smiled—"my wife, Alana, is pregnant. I think . . . I think Dad knew. The last time the lawyer was out at the farm Alana was still dealing with morning sickness. It wouldn't have been hard to figure out that she was pregnant. I kind of hope Dad did know. I hope it made him happy. Nothing else about me did."

William was wearing a gold signet ring on his right hand and he twisted it around his finger. "I've learned something about money that maybe my father figured out just a little too late: It can buy happiness *if* you know how to spend it."

We thanked him for talking to us, found Mac and made our way back to the car.

"That's what he meant when he asked his driver about first loves and roads not taken," I said to Rose as I unlocked her door.

"You think Vincent knew he was going to be a grandfather."

"I do. And I think maybe it made him want to fix

his mistakes. Do you remember what the driver told us? He said, 'I told him there was no point in wasting time on what's already done.' And Mr. Swift said, 'Wouldn't you want to know for certain?'"

Rose gave me a sad smile. "If you're right, I'm sorry he ran out of time."

Chapter 20

The next morning was the busiest Saturday morning we'd had at Second Chance in weeks. People were coming and going and it seemed everyone who walked through the door bought something.

"I think we could open a shop and sell just those pillows Jess makes," Charlotte said when we finally got a break just after noon.

"And old LPs," I added.

"Why is everybody buying candleholders?" Avery asked. She had gotten the broom and was sweeping up the sand that had been tracked in.

"Valentine's Day," I said. "The same thing happened last year. By the thirteenth we won't have a single one in the shop."

"Is it the same people buying them year after year or different people?"

I returned a guitar to the wall. "I don't know. It's one of the great mysteries of life."

Mr. P. came in from his office then. What little hair he had was sticking out all over his head and a frown knotted his forehead. He handed me some change. "I'm going to make some copies," he said. "Our printer isn't working and I don't have time at the moment to troubleshoot."

"Go ahead," I said. There was no point in telling him—again—that the Angels didn't need to reimburse me for occasionally using my printer. We'd had the conversation more than once and I never won.

"Frustrating morning, Alfred?" Charlotte asked as she reorganized what was left of our vinyl record collection.

"Somewhat." He nudged his glasses up his nose. "We're not getting any security footage from the library."

"Why not?" I said. "I know Ann seemed to be stalling Rose, but I didn't think she'd refuse outright."

"She didn't. Ann finally admitted there is no footage because the camera has been broken for weeks and there's no money in the budget to get it fixed."

"Well, that bites," Avery said.

Mr. P. nodded. "Yes, it does."

Avery swept the last bit of sand into the dustpan, opened the door and dumped it outside. "How about I make tea?"

"That's a lovely idea," Charlotte said. "Thank you."

"So what do we do now?" I said to Mr. P.

"Maybe one of the nearby buildings has a security camera that shows the same part of the street. I'll see what I can find."

He started for the stairs. "Oh, I talked to Dad last night," I called after him. "He said to tell you if there's any information you think he might be able to find to let him know."

My father was a former journalist and still had a lot of sources.

Mr. P. smiled over his shoulder at me. "I appreciate that," he said. "I may take Peter up on that."

It had been good to talk to Mom and Dad but it had also made me miss them. I'd decided that as soon as the case was over, I was going to take Mac's suggestion and go see them for a few days.

Charlotte got to her feet. She walked over to me. "Don't frown like that," she said. "You'll get wrinkles."

I smiled at her. "When I was little, you used to tell me my face would freeze that way if I didn't stop frowning."

She put her arm around my shoulder. "You didn't frown very much. Nicolas, on the other hand . . ." She shook her head.

I laughed. "He had such a temper when we were kids. I kept waiting for his face to freeze in one of those awful grimaces he used to make. I was always kind of disappointed that it didn't happen."

"My mother used to tell me my hair would go curly if I ate my crusts." She gave her head a shake. "That didn't happen, either, but you *will* get wrinkles if you don't stop frowning, so stop."

I laid my head on her shoulder for a moment. "Why can't we figure out who Henry saw? It has to be the same person Brent saw as well."

"We will," Charlotte said. "We just need a little more time. You just talked to him yesterday."

"Am I obsessing?"

She held up her thumb and index finger about a half an inch apart. "Maybe a little bit." She gave my shoulders a squeeze. "Henry could be wrong. He wasn't wearing his glasses. Brent thinks he saw a woman but he can't be sure. And it was very convenient for the killer that the security camera wasn't working and the light was burned out."

"I know," I said.

"You know the person both men saw could have been anyone. That person might not have been following Mr. Swift. That person might not have even been a woman. All we know for sure is that Henry saw someone with hair and a coat similar to Stella's walk down the street in the same direction Vincent Swift had taken. Brent didn't even notice that much detail. That kind of evidence wouldn't stand up in court. Nor should it. It's flimsier than a wet sheet of tissue paper."

I knew Charlotte was right. I also knew I needed an answer. Had anyone else seen the mystery person? Maybe it was worth asking Earle. Maybe he'd gotten up to stretch his legs. Maybe he'd looked outside. Maybe he'd seen someone. That was a lot of maybes.

Cleveland showed up with Mac's record player needle about half an hour later. I hurried out to the old garage, not even stopping to grab my jacket. "I have something for you," I said. I handed him a shiny kettle with a copper bottom. "It whistles," I said. "Tell Memphis it's a housewarming present."

Cleveland grinned. "Thank you. I will."

"And could you ask Earle a question for me?"

"Sure," he said.

"After he saw Mr. Swift leave the library, did he see anyone else leaving?"

He nodded. "I'll let you know."

I was busy with customers for the next couple hours. Mr. P. came in around three thirty. "I have a message from Cleveland. He said to tell you Earle remembered that right after he saw Mr. Swift leave he got up to get a drink of water. He didn't see anyone else go out, but he could have missed someone." He studied my face. "Does that make sense to you?"

"It does," I said. "Thank you."

I went out to the workroom. Mac had the drawer from the desk I'd bought from Cleveland in pieces on the workbench. "Could you cover for me in the shop for a little while?" I asked. "I need to hit the paint store to get some color swatches for the mantel."

"Avery put all our paint swatches on a binder ring, remember?" he said. "They're on the bottom shelf of paint cans."

"I need fresh ones," I said.

Mac set down the tiny pair of pliers he was holding. "Where are you really going?"

I smoothed a hand over my hair. "I don't know. I just need some fresh air and a few minutes without Rose *and* Charlotte *and* Mr. P. all being the voices of reason in my ear."

Mac slid off his stool. "Go," he said. "I've got this."

I went. I actually stopped and bought a sample pot of a creamy white shade of paint I thought might work on the mantel. And then, somehow, I found myself at the library. I wasn't really sure what I was doing there. I'd had a vague idea that maybe I could talk to some of the staff, but once I was in the building I could see how silly that idea was. I turned around to leave and spotted Teresa Reynard. I remembered what Rose had said about the picker being at the library a lot. Had she been there on Monday night?

Teresa spotted me and raised one hand, her way of saying hello. I walked over to her. She was a couple of inches shorter than me, with wide shoulders and strong, solid legs. She wore a quilted navy blue parka and heavy lace-up winter boots. Her long, curly hair was pulled back in a loose ponytail and I could see the end of a pair of black earmuffs hanging out of one of her pockets. I was guessing her van, which she called Mitch, was in the parking lot.

"Hello, Sarah. What are you doing here?" she said. "I've never seen you here on a Saturday."

"I'm usually at the shop on Saturdays," I said.

She nodded. "I know. So why are you here today?"

Teresa wasn't really any good at social niceties. She was plainspoken and honest to a fault. I liked her. You never had to guess what she thought about someone or something because she'd tell you.

"The Angels have a new case," I said. "They're trying to find out who killed a man named Vincent Swift."

"I know who that is," she said.

"Teresa, were you here Monday night?"

She shook her head. "No, I wasn't here."

I felt a twist of disappointment. I'd known it was a long shot.

"Monday is coding night," she said. "I'm learning to code."

"That's good," I said.

Teresa smiled. "Yes, it is. I like the class because it's all women and there are no stupid men trying to get me to go out with them. Mr. Swift was arguing with Stella Hall on Monday night. You probably already know that. They were loud and we all heard them. He was a bully."

I held up one hand. "Wait a minute. How did you hear them if you were in your class?"

She looked at me as though I was missing something obvious. "The class is upstairs in the big meeting room."

"You said you weren't at the library on Monday."

Teresa shook her head. "No, I didn't. You asked if I was here." She gestured at the floor with both hands. "I wasn't here. I was upstairs."

I took a deep breath. I knew how literal Teresa could be. I should have been more specific.

"I'm sorry. I did say that." I took a moment wondering how to word my next question. "You heard Stella arguing. Did you see her then or later?"

"No."

"Did you see Mr. Swift then or later?"

"No," she said again.

"When you left after your class, did you go out the front door?"

Teresa shook her head. "I came down the stairs and used the side door. I don't like elevators because there are generally too many people and poor ventilation. And taking the stairs is better exercise."

I nodded. "You're right."

"I know," she said.

"When you got outside did you see anyone on the street between the library and the corner?" My breath seemed to be caught in my chest.

"Yes. I saw a person with light hair and a light brown coat. I couldn't tell the person's gender because they were too far away and because the streetlight by the front doors isn't working. I complained about it two weeks ago but no one has fixed it yet."

I could feel something sour at the back of my throat. "Could the person you saw have been Stella?" I asked.

Teresa shook her head again. "No. I told you I didn't see Stella on Monday night. Did you forget?"

"I guess I did," I said. "I'm sorry. How do you know it wasn't Stella?"

"The person I saw was taller. Stella is short. I estimate she's just over five feet tall."

I nodded.

"And she would have been hunched over because it was very cold Monday night."

I nodded again.

"Then it couldn't have been her because Stella's head would have been level with the point where the base of the lamppost narrows."

I looked blankly at her.

"I'll show you," she said.

We went outside and Teresa led us over to one of the decorative lampposts that lined the street. "See? The spot where the base narrows is several inches below the tops of our heads because we're taller than Stella."

"Okay," I said.

"The lampposts are all thirteen feet high." She pointed to the light at the top well above our heads. "That base section is just over five feet, which I can tell by estimating what fraction of the total it is. Stella's head would have been level with the top of the base. The person I saw was taller. Does that help?"

"Yes," I said. "It does."

I sat in my car in the parking lot and thought about the people we'd talked to in the last few days. I thought about who, in the end, had the most compelling reason to want Vincent Swift dead. My stomach hurt.

I drove back to the shop.

Rose was just bringing Mr. P. a cup of coffee. She took one look at my face and said. "What's wrong?"

"I think I know who did it," I said.

I told them what Teresa had told me. I repeated what Henry had said about the person he'd seen, that he'd believed to be Stella: fair hair and light brown coat.

"Maybe I'm taking a leap in logic but it feels right to me. I just don't want to tell Michelle until I'm sure. Maybe because part of me wants to be wrong."

Rose nodded. "Alfred will go with you," she said. "Won't you?"

"Of course I will," he said. He patted my arm and put on his coat.

I wanted him to tell me there was something

wrong with my conclusion, that I'd made a misstep in my reasoning. But he didn't.

Mr. P. and I made the short drive across town in silence. We pulled up in front of the Telfers' redbrick Victorian. The house had been beautifully restored. The front door and the trim around the window were painted black. A wrought-iron picketed fence outlined a small front garden sleeping under the snow.

Natalie was just coming along the sidewalk, head down, hands stuffed in the pockets of her jacket. She looked up as Mr. P. and I got out of the SUV. We walked over to her and I introduced Mr. P.

"Have you been waiting very long?" she asked.

I shook my head. "No. We just got here."

"I saw you at the library earlier. I guessed that you'd be waiting for me."

I let the silence hang between us for a long moment before I spoke, knowing once I did, there would be no taking the words back.

"You killed Vincent Swift," I said at last.

Natalie nodded. "Yes, I did."

Chapter 21

"Could we go inside?" I asked.

Natalie nodded again. She led the way up the brick walkway, stopping to unlock the front door.

The house was just as beautiful inside as it was outside, with high ceilings, gleaming wood floors and lots of light. Natalie led us into what I guessed had been the parlor at one time.

She gestured at the sofa. It was a deep green velvet with wide, rolled arms. Like every other piece of furniture in the room, it didn't look as though it was ever used. "Please . . . have a seat," she said. She remained on her feet, arms wrapped her midsection. I got the sense that now that she'd told someone she wanted to get the details out.

"How did you know?" she asked me.

"I didn't, at first," I said. "But in the end it came down to two things. Out of everyone we talked to, you had the strongest reason for wanting Vincent Swift dead. The two men who lost their jobs after the lawsuit were getting their lives together. They weren't going to kill him and ruin that. He was trying to damage Judge Halloran's reputation but it really wasn't working. Everyone knows the kind of man the judge is. Swift even tried to sandbag the judge's assistant and that didn't work.

"No one really believed Stella could have killed him unless she'd had some sort of blackout. Yes, they'd had more than one loud and public argument about the money the library was getting, but they'd been on opposite sides of a lot of issues. This time wasn't any different. It wasn't enough of a motive."

"I didn't want her to be blamed," Natalie said.

"I know you didn't," I said. "You didn't want Damian to be blamed, either. You told me, *I know he didn't kill Vincent Swift.* I didn't think anything about your choice of words at the time. But you did know. Because it was you."

She nodded. Her eyes shone with unshed tears. "I tried to forgive. I tried to forgive both of them, especially Jacob. I tried not to give in to my urge to make someone pay for what had happened to my child."

Tears slid down her cheek and she swiped at them with one free hand. "I was drowning. Madison loved Jacob so I worked hard to forgive him. But I was still so angry inside."

I swallowed back my own tears. "What changed? What was different about Monday night?"

"I was at the library for an event to promote organ donation. When Madison died, Damian and I . . . donated her organs. You already know that Damian left. It was just too much for him. I got to meet the young man who received one of her corneas." She cleared her throat and her voice was a little stronger. "I was . . . I was so happy for him. He can see now. It was the sort of thing Madison would have loved, but it reminded me that she's gone. I had to step outside for a moment. A woman followed me to see if I was all right. She told me her name was Katherine Brown. The name probably doesn't mean anything to you, does it?"

I shook my head. "I'm sorry. No."

"I didn't know who she was, either," Natalie said. "She's a nurse. And she was the first person to come upon the accident. She was driving right behind them. She tried . . . to save Madison. I had so many questions."

She stopped, pressing her lips together.

"It's okay," I said. "Take your time."

"She, uh, she said the SUV was upside down. Mr. Swift had gotten out and he was slumped against the side of the vehicle. She saw Jacob crawl out of the left-side window and collapse on the ground."

I saw a flash of understanding in Mr. P.'s expression.

"You don't get it, do you?" Natalie said to me.

I shook my head. I didn't.

"She saw the young man crawl out of the *left* side of the SUV," Mr. P. said.

Natalie nodded. "I asked her to repeat herself, and she said she saw Jacob crawl out of the driver's side window." Her eyes were locked on my face. "But that wasn't what she said."

Suddenly I understood the significance of the nurse's words.

"I just walked away from her. All I could think about was that the car had been upside down, which meant if Jacob crawled out of the left-side window he got out on the passenger side, *not* the driver's side. *He wasn't driving.*" She shook her head. "I don't even know how I got downstairs. I didn't know Mr. Swift was even in the building. But there he was. I tried to get his attention but I couldn't seem to find my voice. I saw him bump into a display and knock things to the floor but he didn't stop. I was on autopilot. I began to pick things up. I heard a staff member say she had told Mr. Swift that his driver hadn't returned but he'd said he was going to walk. I knew he was the one person who might be able to tell me whether Jacob was driving the night of the accident."

"So you followed him," I said.

She nodded. "I left the building without realizing I was still holding the fortune-teller's ball I'd picked up. I saw him just turning the corner and I went after him. He wasn't walking very fast so it was easy to catch up with him. I could tell from his face he knew who I was."

Part of me wanted to tell her to stop, that whatever she'd done she'd paid for in advance when her child died.

She swallowed a couple of times. "I told him what Katherine had told me. I asked him to search his memory for any detail about the accident. I expected him to say what he'd said before—that he had no memory of the crash or anything that had happened before it. At first, he didn't say anything. Then he finally looked me in the eye and he said, 'I'm sorry.' He hung his head like he was ashamed and I just knew. I knew that he remembered. And I knew that *he* was driving, not Jacob."

Tears slid down her face again. "I was so angry," she whispered, both arms dropping to her sides. "He killed Madison. He let Jacob get blamed. Those men lost their jobs, and it was all him." She raised one hand and let it fall again. "I hit him. I don't know how many times. I don't remember doing it but suddenly he was on the ground. I didn't think. I didn't try to help him. I just ran."

Part of me wished I could give her absolution. She hadn't gotten justice when Madison died. But Vincent Swift deserved justice just as much as Natalie did. And so did Stella.

I reached over and caught both of her hands in mine. "I'm so, so sorry," I said.

She looked at me for a long moment and then she nodded. "Somebody please . . . call the police," she said in a small voice.

I glanced over my shoulder at Mr. P. and he nodded. He moved several steps away from us and pulled out his cell phone. Natalie was shaking. I folded both of my arms around her as she started to cry. After a moment I felt Mr. P.'s hand on my shoulder and I cried, too.

Chapter 22

I don't know what Mr. P. said to Michelle but she let Damian come home and drive Natalie to the police station. Natalie seemed . . . calmer, a long way from better, but maybe starting down the road to there. Somehow, finally telling someone what had happened had helped her.

"Please tell Stella I'm sorry," she said. She was very pale, but she wasn't shaking any longer and some of the haunted look was gone from her eyes. Damian had his arm around her shoulders.

"I will," I said. "And I know she would tell you to just take care of yourself. I'm going to be checking up on you to make sure you do."

I drove Mr. P. back to the shop. "I have to go see Liz," I said to him as we pulled into the parking lot.

He reached over and gave my hand a squeeze. He didn't ask any questions. All he said was, "Go."

I drove over to the Emmerson Foundation offices. Jane Evans took one look at me and sent me in to Liz's office. I told her about Natalie. Her jaw tightened and lines pulled at the corners of her mouth. She got to her feet and walked around the desk. "What do you need?" she asked. "What does Natalie need?"

"You," I said. I held out one hand. "I need *this* you. I need Elizabeth Emmerson Kiley French. I need your influence and your connections. I know that Natalie killed Vincent Swift and she can't just walk away from that. She isn't trying to. But it was what he did, the lies he told, that set everything else in motion, including his own death. I want Natalie to have . . . hope. Please."

"Done," she said.

I felt some of the tightness in my chest ease. I wrapped my arms around her and rested my head on her shoulder. "I love you," I said.

She leaned her head against mine. "I love you, too, sweet pea," she said.

On Monday morning, I went down to the library. I found Stella scraping gum from underneath a table in the children's department. "Did you ever stick your gum under the table when you were a kid?" she asked.

"Isabel Grayson was my grandmother," I said. "What do you think?"

She smiled. "Are you here to see me?"

I nodded. "You said you wished you'd gone back to talk to Mr. Swift the night he died. You wanted to know what he wanted to say to you. I think I know. I think he wanted to tell you that he was going to be a grandfather."

Stella looked confused. "Why would he want to tell me?"

"I can't be certain, but I think he had a couple of reasons. One, I think he was regretting his choices. Maybe it's wishful thinking on my part, but I think he wanted to change. And two, as far as I know, you were the only person he tried to share that news with. I think he still thought of you as his friend."

Stella stared out the window for a moment. Then she sighed and looked at me again. "I wish he'd shown that a little sooner."

"So do I," I said.

Avery unveiled her Valentine's Day window a week before the day. We all trooped out to the front of the store, huddled in our jackets, to see it. She made us all face the street while she took down the paper that had covered the glass for the previous couple of hours. Then she knocked on the window and we all turned around.

It wasn't what I'd been expecting.

The scene was set for a romantic dinner complete with twinkle lights and sparkly red hearts hanging from the ceiling. At a table for two in the center, with candles and champagne, were two stuffed . . . muskrats holding hands (paws). They were both wearing red-framed, heart-shaped glasses. And they looked like they were gazing into each other's eyes. Avery had written "Love Is" in elegant calligraphy script on the glass and in the background the Captain and Tennille song "Muskrat Love" was playing.

"Those muskrats look like a pair of giant rats," Liz muttered beside me. I glared at her. "I'm not going to say that to Avery," she said crossly.

On my other side Mac was already humming. "I'm not going to be able to get that song out of my head," he said with a grin.

Avery came out the front door, hugging herself against the cold because she'd forgotten her jacket. "Well? What do you think?" she asked.

"I think it's perfect," I said.

Avery leaned sideways to look at her grandmother. "Nonna?"

"Great job, kiddo," Liz said. Then she started to clap. Mr. P. immediately did the same, and then we were all clapping and Avery's smile couldn't have gotten any bigger.

We trooped back inside for cake. "Where did you find the muskrats?" Mr. P. asked.

I wasn't sure I wanted to know.

"There's this guy who used to be a taxidermist in Rockport—well, I guess technically he still is. Anyway, he was selling some stuff on Facebook and I saw the muskrats in the background of a photo and of course I thought Muskrat Love, right?"

Mr. P. smiled. "Right," he said.

"Except the guy wouldn't sell them to me. He's kind of a jerk." She looked at her grandmother. "Sorry, but he is."

"But you got the animals," I said. "How did you convince him?"

She shrugged. "I asked him what he wanted. He said he wanted this particular Furby thing for his collection. I found someone who had it and then I did a trade. That's why I asked if I could have that old chandelier."

"You traded that old light fixture for a Furby?" I said.

Avery shook her head. "I traded the chandelier for an old record player. I traded the record player for a really old Monopoly game." She brushed her hair back off her face. "I traded *that* for a purple vinyl *Purple Rain* promotional album. And I traded the album for the Furby." She looked at me. "Like you did for your house."

I smiled. "I'm impressed."

The window was a big hit with customers. On Valentine's Day, we had a constant stream of people coming in the store to say how much they liked it and most of them ended up buying something.

At twelve thirty, Mac came in from outside. "I need you to come out and look at something," he said.

"Okay," I said. I turned to Avery. "I'll be right back."

She shrugged. "Sure."

We walked across the parking lot and when we got to the door of the old garage he leaned over and kissed my cheek. I stepped inside to find the space filled with people. Gram held out her hands and said, "Happy Valentine's Day!"

She and John were there and so were Rose and Mr. P., Charlotte, Liz, Jess, Michelle, Nick, even Liam and Mom and Dad. Avery had slipped in behind me carrying Elvis.

I looked at Mac. "I don't understand. What is this?"

"Valentine's Day is about love, and that's what I wanted to give you: Here are all the people you love the most. Sorry, I don't think any of them are returnable."

I was overcome with emotion. For a moment I just stood there unsure whether tears or laughter was going to win. Then I hugged him. "Best Valentine's gift ever," I whispered in his ear.

"This might be *the* most romantic thing ever," Avery said.

I hugged her. "You helped, didn't you?"

She ducked her head. "Maybe a little."

"I love you, you know."

"I know," she said. Then she smiled. "I love you, too."

I hugged Mom and Dad and teased Mom for not giving anything away when we'd talked over the weekend.

"Where did everyone park?" I asked.

"That's what you need to know?" Liz said.

I grinned. "I love you."

She rolled her eyes. "Yeah, yeah, everyone does."

Rose had made a gorgeous heart-shaped cake, which she was already cutting into slices. She blew me a kiss and I blew one back to her.

Jess made her way over to me. "See?" she said. "What did I tell you? This is all you need for Valentine's Day. A little love and a little chocolate."

I narrowed my eyes at her. "When I was whining, you already knew what Mac had planned, didn't you?"

She made an elaborate and very fake shrug. "Maybe."

She looked over at Mac, who was talking to Gram. "He's going to love your present."

"You think so?" I asked.

"I know so," she said.

Nick came up behind her. "Rose wants us to pass out cake," he said.

She grinned and slugged his arm. "Then let's do it."

"Have fun tonight," I said.

"I'm planning on it," Jess said. "You, too."

That night after dinner, I gave Mac his gift.

"It's not as perfect as your present was, but I hope you like it." I handed him an envelope.

He opened it and pulled out a photo. "It's a picture of a garage," he said. It was clear he was confused and trying not to show it.

"It's *your* garage for the next six months," I said. "I rented it from Memphis. It's out behind the house he bought. It's insulated. And there's lots of light. Memphis installed a security system he'll have to explain, and the space is more than big enough to build a boat."

Mac looked from the photo to me. It was the first time I'd ever known him to be speechless.

"You've given all of your time to the shop," I said, "and to me, and to everyone else. And now it's time to starting building the dream you had when you came to North Harbor." I looked at him. "Was that too hokey?"

He shook his head. "No. It was just right."

*   *   *

The next morning, I went out for a very early run. I was determined that my legs wouldn't feel like two bags of jelly the next time I went skating. I was almost at Jess's place when I saw someone coming out of her door. A male someone. His head was down, his hair rumpled, and half of the collar of his coat was stuck down inside the neck. Jess must have had a good Valentine's Day, I thought.

Then I realized the man I was looking at was Nick.

Acknowledgments

Well-deserved thanks, as always, go to my agent, Kim Lionetti; my editor, Jessica Wade; and everyone at Berkley whose efforts always make me look good.

Thanks as well to all the librarians who encourage readers of all ages and who champion so many authors, including me.

And last, but never least, thank you to Patrick and Lauren, who are my happy ending!

Love Elvis the cat?
Then meet Hercules and Owen!
Read on for an excerpt from
the first book by Sofie Kelly
in the Magical Cats Mysteries . . .

CURIOSITY THRILLED THE CAT

Available in paperback
from Berkley Prime Crime!

The body was smack in the middle of my freshly scrubbed kitchen floor. Fred the Funky Chicken, minus his head.

"Owen!" I said sharply.

Nothing.

"Owen, you little fur ball, I know you did this. Where are you?"

There was a muffled "meow" from the back door. I leaned around the cupboards. Owen was sprawled on his back in front of the screen door, a neon yellow feather sticking out of his mouth. He rolled over onto his side and looked at me with the same goofy expression I used to get from stoned students coming into the BU library.

I crouched down next to the gray-and-white tabby. "Owen, you killed Fred," I said. "That's the third chicken this week."

The cat sat up slowly and stretched. He padded over to me and put one paw on my knee. Tipping his head to one side he looked up at me with his golden eyes. I sat back against the end of the cupboard. Owen climbed onto my lap and put his two front paws on my chest. The feather was still sticking out of his mouth.

I held out my right hand. "Give me Fred's head," I said. The cat looked at me unblinkingly. "C'mon, Owen. Spit it out."

He turned his head sideways and dropped what was left of Fred the Funky Chicken's head into my hand. It was a soggy lump of cotton with that lone yellow feather stuck on the end.

"You have a problem, Owen," I told the cat. "You have a monkey on your back." I dropped what was left of the toy's head onto the floor and wiped my hand on my gray yoga pants. "Or maybe I should say you have a chicken on your back."

The cat nuzzled my chin, then laid his head against my T-shirt, closed his eyes and started to purr.

I stroked the top of his head. "That's what they all say," I told him. "You're addicted, you little fur ball, and Rebecca is your dealer."

Owen just kept on purring and ignored me. Hercules came around the corner then. "Your brother is a catnip junkie," I said to the little tuxedo cat.

Hercules climbed over my legs and sniffed the remains of Fred the Funky Chicken's head. Then he looked at Owen, rumbling like a diesel engine as I scratched the side of his head. I swear there was disdain on Hercules's furry face. Stick catnip in, on or near anything and Owen squirmed with joy. Hercules, on the other hand, was indifferent.

The stocky black-and-white cat climbed onto my

lap, too. He put one white paw on my shoulder and swatted at my hair.

"Behind the ear?" I asked.

"Meow," the cat said.

I took that as a yes, and tucked the strands back behind my ear. I was used to long hair, but I'd cut mine several months ago. I was still adjusting to the change in style. At least I hadn't given in to the impulse to dye my dark brown hair blond.

"Maybe I'll ask Rebecca if she has any ideas for my hair," I said. "She's supposed to be back tonight." At the sound of Rebecca's name Owen lifted his head. He'd taken to Rebecca from the first moment he'd seen her, about two weeks after I'd brought the cats home.

Both Owen and Hercules had been feral kittens. I'd found them, or more truthfully they'd found me, about a month after I'd arrived in town. I had no idea how old they were. They were affectionate with me, but wouldn't allow anyone else to come near them, let alone touch them. That hadn't stopped Rebecca, my backyard neighbor, from trying. She'd been buying both cats little catnip toys for weeks now, but all she'd done was turn Owen into a chicken-decapitating catnip junkie. She was on vacation right now, but Owen had clearly managed to unearth a chicken from a secret stash somewhere.

I stroked the top of his head again. "Go back to sleep," I said. "You're going cold turkey . . . or maybe I should say cold chicken. I'm telling Rebecca no more catnip toys for you. You're getting lazy."

Owen put his head down again, while Hercules used his to butt my free hand. "You want some attention, too?" I asked. I scratched the spot, almost at the top of his head, where the white fur around his mouth and up the bridge of his nose gave way to black. His green eyes narrowed to slits and he began to purr, as well. The rumbling was kind of like being in the service bay of a Volkswagen dealership.

I glanced up at the clock. "Okay, you two. Let me up. It's almost time for me to go and I have to take care of the dearly departed before I do."

I'd sold my car when I'd moved to Minnesota from Boston, and because I could walk everywhere in Mayville Heights, I still hadn't bought a new one. Since I had no car, I'd spent my first few weeks in town wandering around exploring, which is how I'd stumbled on Wisteria Hill, the abandoned Henderson estate. Everett Henderson had hired me at the library.

Owen and Hercules had peered out at me from a tumble of raspberry canes and then followed me around while I explored the overgrown English country garden behind the house. I'd seen several other full-grown cats, but they'd all disappeared as soon as I got anywhere close to them. When I left, Owen and Hercules followed me down the rutted gravel driveway. Twice I'd picked them up and carried them back to the empty house, but that didn't deter them. I looked everywhere, but I couldn't find their mother. They were so small and so determined to come with me that in the end I'd brought them home.

There were whispers around town about Wisteria Hill and the feral cats. But that didn't mean there was anything unusual about my cats. Oh no, nothing unusual at all. It didn't matter that I'd heard rumors about strange lights and ghosts. No one had lived at the estate for quite a while, but Everett refused to sell it or do anything with the property. I'd heard that he'd grown up at Wisteria Hill. Maybe that was why he didn't want to change anything.

Speaking of not wanting change, Hercules was not eager to relinquish his prime spot on my lap. But after some gentle prodding, he shook himself and got off. Owen yawned a couple of times, stretched and took twice as long to move.

I got the broom and dustpan from the porch and swept up the remains of Fred the Funky Chicken. Owen and Hercules sat in front of the refrigerator and watched. Owen made a move toward the dustpan, like he was toying with the idea of grabbing the body and making a run for it.

I glared at him. "Don't even think about it."

He sat back down, making low, grumbling meows in his throat.

I flipped open the lid of the garbage can and held the pan over the top. "Fred was a good chicken," I said solemnly. "He was a funky chicken and we'll miss him."

"Meow," Owen yowled.

I flipped what was left of the catnip toy into the garbage. "Rest in peace, Fred," I said as the lid closed.

I put the broom away, brushed the cat hair off my shirt and washed my hands. I looked in the bathroom mirror. Hercules was right. My hair did look better tucked behind my ear.

My messenger bag with a towel and canvas shoes for tai chi class was in the front closet. I set it by the door and went back through the house to make sure the cats had fresh water.

"I'm leaving," I said. But both cats had disappeared and I didn't get any answer.

I stopped to grab my keys and pick up my bag. Locking the door behind me, I headed out, down Mountain Road.

The sun was yellow-orange, low on the sky over Lake Pepin. It was a warm Minnesota evening, without the sticky humidity of Boston in late July. I shifted my bag from one shoulder to the other. I wasn't going to think about Boston. Minnesota was home now—at least for the next eighteen months or so.

The street curved in toward the center of town as I headed down the hill, and the roof of the library building came into view below. It sat on the midpoint of a curve of shoreline, protected from the water by a rock wall. The brick building had a stained-glass window that dominated one end and a copper-roofed cupola, complete with its original wrought-iron weather vane.

The Mayville Heights Free Public Library was a Carnegie library, built in 1912 with money donated by the industrialist and philanthropist Andrew Carnegie. Now it was being restored and updated to celebrate its centenary. That was why I had been in town for the last several months. And why I'd be here for the next year and a half. I was supervising the restoration—which was almost finished—as well as updating the collections, computerizing the card catalog and setting up free internet access for the library patrons. I was slowly learning the reading history of everyone in town. It made me feel like I knew the people a little, as well.

ABOUT THE AUTHOR

Sofie Ryan is a writer and mixed-media artist who loves to repurpose things in her life and in her art. She is the author of *Totally Pawstruck*, *Claw Enforcement*, and *No Escape Claws* in the *New York Times* bestselling Second Chance Cat Mysteries. She also writes the *New York Times* bestselling Magical Cats Mysteries under the name Sofie Kelly.

CONNECT ONLINE

SofieRyan.com